STONE HAVEN: MURDER ALONG THE RIVER

STONE HAVEN: MURDER ALONG THE RIVER

•

Holly Fox Vellekoop

AVALON BOOKS
NEW YORK

Published by Thomas Bouregy & Co., Inc.
160 Madison Avenue, New York, NY 10016

Library of Congress Cataloging-in-Publication Data

Vellekoop, Holly Fox.
    Stone haven : murder along the river / Holly Fox Vellekoop.
        p. cm.
    ISBN 0-8034-9779-2 (alk. paper)
    I. Title.

PS3622.E55S76 2006
813'.6—dc22

                                        2005037649

PRINTED IN THE UNITED STATES OF AMERICA
ON ACID-FREE PAPER
BY HADDON CRAFTSMEN, BLOOMSBURG, PENNSYLVANIA

I would like to thank Trooper Marlin Foulds,
Trooper Kevin Kearney, both of the Pennsylvania
State Police, and Thomas L. Isenberg, Retired
Pennsylvania State Police Officer, for their assistance
in some technical aspects of this mystery.

I dedicate this book to my loving husband, Ronald Vellekoop, who encouraged me every step of the way.

And

To all the men and women of the United States military who are serving their country around the world.

Prologue

Even in death, you knew that Rose Stone, the fifty-two-year-old wife of psychiatrist Dr. Lesley Stone, came from money, married money, and died in a setting of wealth. Rose's petite body, a body familiar to expensive wrappings, was sprawled indecently in front of the white marble kitchen sink. Her short, ash blond hair framed a Tyrolean face, flaccid and unseeing at this hideous death scene. A trickle of blood outlined the fold of her left cheek and trailed down her carotid artery.

The expensive black Guccis were not on Rose's size-six, perfectly pedicured feet. Instead, one lay on the white Italian marble floor of the largest, most elaborate kitchen Lana Stahl had ever seen. The other blood-spattered shoe nestled next to Rose's lifeless body, which was clad in a black Armani pantsuit.

Shards of what appeared to have been a glass figurine were splayed about the floor, mingling with the

1

cooling blood. Looking closely, one could see the glass remnants of the statue's perfectly coifed head, the pale orange and blue fragments obscenely reflecting the still moist bodily fluids of Danville's richest woman.

Rose was wearing no jewelry. Not even a watch or earrings. *How strange,* thought Lana, eyebrows furrowing; *Rose's diamond ring is gone.*

The diamond in the setting was the well-known Darling Diamond, a nine carat square cut, flawless white diamond set in platinum. Rose always wore it on her right hand. The hand she used to gesture with as she talked animatedly about her many subjects of interest.

You couldn't help but look at the ring. Everyone looked at that ring when Rose was near. That's how compelling it was. But there was nothing there to look at now, nothing but blood and lifeless money.

Lana forced herself to turn away from the grisly sight, a stark contrast to the stainless steel appliances complementing the white and black designer kitchen layout. A layout that was not planned for the violence that had played out earlier this Friday afternoon.

Fear began to seize her as she gazed about the room. Paralyzing fear. She thought once or twice that she was going to be ill, and held a tissue to her face and gagged. She tried not to look at the dead body, but her eyes kept coming back to Rose.

Almost thirty years of nursing had prepared her for a lot of things, but not for this. As a psychiatric nurse, Lana had seen violence and blood. She had witnessed the borderline's self-mutilations, which could turn stomachs. Paper clips or staples pushed into arms clean to the bone, eventually rendering the limb useless. Self-inflicted scars across the torso from knees to shoulders, so dense that you couldn't tell where one ended and the other began. All this in some attempt to assuage one's inner anxiety and torment.

There was even the time that Kendra, a chronic schizophrenic, performed self-enucleation by pulling her myopic left eye from its socket and devouring it in full view of shocked observers in a locked ward day-room. As horrible as that was, it did not compare to what Lana had stumbled onto today.

Nurses see death at times and, while it is always difficult, it is sometimes expected. This was unexpected and affected Lana on a different level. She was in shock from a recognition of the depravity of the killer of this woman.

Lana was frantic, and gasping for breath due to fear, distress . . . and the stench of blood. Her heart pounding violently in her chest, she rushed out the door. She half-ran, half-stumbled to her car, with nary a glance at her surroundings. Digging wildly through her purse, Lana came up with the keys to unlock the passenger door. She fumbled and dropped them, grabbed them off the driveway, then dropped them again. Finally, still shaking, she was able to unlock the car door, get in, and relock it behind her. Leaning down to the floor mat, she reached anxiously for her cell phone and dialed 911.

Chapter One

While the local and state police milled about collecting evidence and cordoning off the crime scene with black and yellow plastic tape in an effort to preserve evidence, Lana sat stoically and silently in the living room, trying to compose herself. A young black state policewoman offered her coffee from a fast food carrier and in a comforting tone, asked her if she needed anything. Lana shook her head no. Before she went back to gathering evidence, the trooper told her it would be just a few minutes before Lieutenant Sheski, an investigator, would come in to speak to her.

Lana looked about at the Stones' costly home. She wasn't the only one impressed. As the police completed their routine tasks, Lana occasionally heard them remarking, "What this place must have cost . . ." and other phrases of admiration.

4

Art deco in design, the white sprawling twenty-one-room mansion stood out amid the expensive two-story colonials and recently-built Victorian-style mansions in the gated Sweetriver development, a cluster of elegant homes that was known for its exclusivity, gated entrance, and impeccable landscaping.

The house had several levels, with cube glass windows and stainless steel and blue glass accents. From the high elevation, multi-tiered balconies looked out over neighboring properties.

Lana had known Dr. and Mrs. Stone since she came to work at Stone Haven, the private hospital the psychiatrist owned and managed. Today was the first time that she had been invited to their home. They usually met at some local restaurant for their discussions, preferring neutral ground to work on mutual community projects. Lana didn't travel in the same social circles as the Stones. Now here she was, sitting on their imported white and gold Italian leather couch, averting her eyes from the doctor's dead wife.

This is horrible, she thought, and said a silent prayer for her dead friend, and for herself.

"Are you okay?"

Lana looked up from where she was sitting into the handsome middle-age face of State Police Lieutenant Tommy Sheski. It was a strong face that validated his heritage.

Sheski was Pennsylvania Dutch on his mother's side and Polish on his father's. His paternal grandparents had emigrated post-war from Poland to the heart of the Pennsylvania coal region. Somewhere en route to

Centralia, Pennsylvania, their long Polish family name became shortened to Sheski.

The trooper had high Polish cheekbones on a broad, attractive face, and stood six foot even, with a thick, strong body. A dark suit, white shirt, and dark tie enhanced his rugged good looks.

"Sure, I'm okay. But can I go soon? I want to go home, I have work to do, my dog is waiting, and . . ." At this point, Lana began to cry softly. Tears streamed down her face.

She couldn't do any work in her condition now even if she wanted to, and she knew it. She thought of the horror she had witnessed. Then her mind wandered to her tiny Yorkshire Terrier, Bunky, waiting for her to feed him his supper. It was now 5:40 P.M. and she was long overdue. Bunky would know she was late and would be waiting expectantly in the laundry room of their century-old Queen Anne house for his owner to come and fill his dish.

Lana's medium-length auburn hair fell around her face, framing big green eyes, reddened and swollen from weeping.

At fifty-two, she looked ten years younger, and the detective softened in response to her good looks and obvious distress. *We men are such wimps about a woman like this,* he thought.

"It won't be long," he responded. "I only have a few questions to ask you right now. We can talk again later."

Sheski turned to one of the many uniformed Pennsylvania State Police officers milling about the scene, and whispered something that Lana could not hear. He then sat down next to her and stared long and hard into her face, shifting his gaze just once to see if she was wearing a wedding set. There was none. He found that interesting.

"Tell me what brought you to the Sweetriver development today," Sheski asked slowly.

"There's not much to tell, Lieutenant."

"Please, call me Tommy," he interrupted.

For some reason he preferred having her call him by his first name, although most people called him by his surname. He tolerated "Sheski" but really hated it when he was referred to as "The Polock."

For now, the state trooper wanted to make Lana comfortable. She was the first person to arrive at the murder scene, and he would need her to relax and feel free to talk. He also wanted to be on a first name basis with her.

Sheski found her attractive and was looking closely at her for more than just professional reasons. She appeared to be educated, and was wearing a gray pantsuit, white cotton shell, and black loafers with a deep, broad heel. He was trying to determine her age, wrongly guessing it in the forties.

Lieutenant Thomas Sheski was a native of Centralia, a Pennsylvania coal town that had its own share of troubles. His hometown, rich in anthracite lore and history, was the unfortunate host of underground fires burning unchecked in anthracite coal veins since the early 1960s. When smoke from the fires began billowing out of the ground, blinding drivers on Route 61 and spewing toxic chemicals, the federal government stepped in. Much to the community's surprise and horror, government officials decided to wipe their coal town off the map. Literally.

A government condemnation and subsequent buyout of Centralia properties was for the residents' own good, officials reported. Sadly, it turned the once charming little town into a big vacant lot with streets. Just a few loyal Centralia inhabitants remain today, their grit and determination an example of Pennsylvania coal town character.

After graduating from high school, Sheski had gone on to Penn State University, nestled in the happy valley of State College, PA, home of the Nittany Lions. He had been heavily recruited for college football. Many colleges and universities appreciate the tough young athletes from the Pennsylvania coal regions. They have a reputation for strength, agility, and endurance. Sheski was no exception.

A dean's list student, he was a first string fullback for two seasons. After graduating with a BS in criminology, he went to the Pennsylvania State Police Academy in Hershey, and on to a career as a state police officer. Coming from this background, he was hard to fool. Life experiences had taught him a lot.

"Well, Tommy," Lana began again, "I was in my office at Stone Haven working on paperwork when it started to get late, so I decided I'd finish it at home." She dabbed at her eyes intermittently with a tissue, speaking in a quiet, soft voice. "I was preparing to leave, and while rummaging through my briefcase, found some bid forms that were supposed to go to the eight P.M. Restoration Committee meeting tonight. I knew I couldn't be there because of my workload, so I called Rose Stone to see if she could take them."

"About what time was that?" Sheski asked.

"That was about three-fifteen. I remember looking at my watch and wondering if she would be home. Rose was a busy woman. She had many interests and was dedicated to the restoration of Danville. Everyone knew about her projects. She really . . ."

At this point, Lana began to sob, her whole body shaking violently. After a few minutes, she wiped her eyes and nose with a crumpled tissue she had been holding, and regained her composure.

"She really wanted to help revive her husband's hometown to its original turn-of-the-century look. Rose often said that the town park would be the beginning. She would bring back its original charm with a water fountain and flower beds. Rose had big plans. Plans that included a total change for Mill Street. When she gained their cooperation, she wanted to have the merchants restore their storefronts to their original Victorian-era charm. It would have been beautiful."

Sheski nodded his head slightly, encouraging her to continue her story. "What happened next?"

"When I told her I still had those bid forms, she asked if I could bring them to her home. The sooner the better. She said she was expecting someone and wanted some time to review the documents for tonight's meeting."

Lana paused, then said thoughtfully, "She sounded a little nervous, for Rose. She was always so composed, so in control. Anyway, when I finished what I had to do, I got into my car and came over."

"About what time did you arrive?"

"It was four-forty P.M. You can ask the gatekeeper about that. When I pulled up to his station, he checked his watch and recorded our encounter in his log book, so I looked at my watch. Rose must have called ahead to him, because when I approached the Sweetriver entrance, he looked at a reference sheet attached to his clipboard and opened the gates so I could go on in. Then he got out of his booth, and as I drove past him, he peered into my car and smiled and waved me on through."

"When you drove through the gates, did you see anyone else walking or driving along the road?" Sheski questioned.

He was looking her in the eyes while he spoke, breaking contact only to take notes.

"No, there was no one. I drove through the development, following Rose's directions, which I had written down. When I came to the end of Montgomery Street, I looked up and there it was. This house. You couldn't miss it. It's the most fascinating home in Sweetriver. I pulled into the driveway, up to the side, and parked. I didn't go right in though, because I wanted to look around for a few minutes. Although I've heard a lot about this place, I've never been here before and just wanted to soak it in."

The Stone's art deco style house was known throughout the state and was frequently photographed by those who could get past the guard or sneak in on the unfinished dirt road behind the property. More than one house-beautiful magazine did a full-color spread on the showplace. It had even been featured on a television show that spotlights homes of the wealthy.

Lana stated that she had taken her time going up to the house, enjoying the beauty. The fifty-foot-long ceramic and glass walk alone was enough to cause even the most jaded to stare at the artwork underfoot.

"Once I arrived, I didn't think that Rose would mind my taking a little time to look around outside. I assumed she would be used to it. After all, there's no other house in our area that even comes close to this. And I love looking at houses."

Lana paused, looked at the detective and asked, "Lieutenant Sheski—Tommy—who could do this? Rose was usually so kind. I know that a lot of people found her to be pushy and ambitious when she wanted something, but she did a lot of good for this town, and she was always nice to me."

Evidently everyone was not as impressed as you seem to be, Sheski mused. *Rose must have pushed someone too far.* In an attempt to keep Lana centered on the sequence of events, he asked laconically, "What happened next?"

Lana recognized his need for her to remain focused.

"After looking at the walkway, I wandered off to the gardens just to the side of the house to get a better look at the grounds. They're wonderful." She emphasized the word *wonderful.*

"Did you see anyone else around the place?"

"Only a man working in the back of the garden by the gate near the road. He looked like a gardener and seemed to be trimming the shrubbery. I didn't look really closely, so I didn't see his face."

"Did he look up at you, smile, wave, or do anything to acknowledge that he had seen you?" Sheski asked.

"No," she puzzled, shaking her head back and forth. "I'm not sure, but I don't think he saw me."

"What did he look like? What was he wearing?" Sheski asked quickly.

"I told you, I didn't look that closely," she said wearily. "I think he had some sort of gardening tool, like the kind that is used to trim shrubbery. It had long handles. He was about my height and, um . . . was wearing old work clothes," she said. "With an unbuttoned flannel shirt over another shirt. That's all I remember. As I told you, I was too busy enjoying the landscape."

Lieutenant Sheski called one of the state policemen over, gave him the details about the man Lana saw in the yard, and asked him to check and see if the Stones had their own gardener.

Sheski turned back to Lana, looked her over, and asked her if she was okay. Did she need a break or anything?

She indicated that she could go on.

"After you looked around the garden, what did you do next?" he asked.

"I went to the side door as Rose had told me to do, rang the doorbell, and waited for someone to answer it. After a minute or so, I shaded my eyes and peeked through the door window to see if anyone was there, but I couldn't see anything. I thought that since Rose had said she was expecting company, maybe she was occupied with her visitor. I waited a few minutes and then rang the doorbell again."

Lana looked away from him, sighed, and bowed her head. Another tear streaked down her pretty cheek. She wiped it away, touched her hair briefly, and continued.

"It was then that I looked through a larger window to the side of the door, and saw her body. I was horrified. All I could think of was maybe, since I'm a nurse, I could still help her. Without thinking about the danger, I tried the door. It was unlocked, so I went inside. My God, what a sight." She leaned her chin on her hand and sighed heavily.

"I was too late. I could see that right away. I checked for breathing and a pulse anyway. There was neither. I touched her arm and it was still warm. That's when I went outside to my car and called 911. I locked the car doors and waited for someone to arrive. I didn't touch anything else, in case you're wondering."

She stopped for a few seconds and looked directly at the detective. Sniffling, she asked, "What happened here?"

"Well," Sheski began, "According to the coroner's first impression, Mrs. Stone was killed instantly by a massive blow to the base of her skull. She never knew what hit her. Her killer then proceeded to repeatedly strike her with a heavy weapon. Someone wanted to make sure the job was thorough. There are multiple blunt force wounds. The attack was savage enough to knock her out of her shoes. And, did you notice, she was well dressed, but wearing no jewelry. By the marks on her body, her rings, earrings, and necklace must have been ripped right off of her. The murderer was one strong individual."

Lana said nothing. She had her eyes closed and her head resting in her left hand as if she was ready to pass out. She started to cry silently.

What a waste, she thought, *what a waste. Rose had a wonderful life and all those plans to improve her community. Now she's gone.*

Sheski's eyes met those of one of the staties standing over the body. They stared at each other, then back at Lana, both unsure of the part their witness really played in this mess. After all, she was the first person on the scene, and as of now, they knew little about her.

Chapter Two

Lana's hometown, Danville, Pennsylvania, began in the eighteenth century as white settlers came to the area. The community's history is rich with stories of the Native Americans who were already there.

Lana was fond of the place of her birth as well as her present home in Riverside, a community just across the bridge. Returning to her hometown when she had was not an option, it was a necessity. She was getting older, and was at a point in her life when she needed to touch base with family and old friends. To be with people she knew and understood, and who cared about her.

As the youngest child in a large family of five girls and one boy, Lana had learned some hard lessons very early in life. Lessons that would prove invaluable to her when, as an adult, she was the charge nurse in a hospital. You did not always get everything you wanted and you worked for what you got. Immediate gratification had yet to come into vogue. However, the longer Lana was in nursing, the more health care became a dollar-driven industry. Although her love for her patients never changed, her view of the wisdom of choosing the industry as a future had.

After her interview with Lieutenant Sheski, Lana drove across the Susquehanna to Riverside and pulled into her carriage house. She got out of the car and went out the back door of the building, locking it behind her.

Still fearful, she rushed up the slate walkway onto the back porch and through the door. When he saw her, Bunky began jumping up and down, staring anxiously at his mistress. He was hungry and she was late with his meal.

Lana bent down to pet her Yorkie, thankful that he was there to greet her. The big house would have been lonely without him.

After serving the tiny dog his supper, Lana took a hot bath. She put on flannel pajamas and a robe and settled into an overstuffed chair to rest with the six-pound dog at her side. "Bunky," she said, looking into the furry, trusting face. "This has been a horrible day." The dog cocked his head as if trying to understand, and snuggled closer to his best friend.

Lana couldn't bring herself to start any of the work she had brought home. It would have to wait. Her mind was reeling with the memory of the crime scene. Blood everywhere, Rose murdered, and her body grotesquely sprawled on the marble floor. She recalled her fears that the killer was still in the Stones' house when she was there, that he knew who she was.

Those fears nagged at her throughout the evening, and she double-checked the five entrances into her old house. She even locked the metal storm doors, something she had never done before. Lana was scared.

Chapter Three

The he state police wasted no time in examining the crime scene. Wealthy, well-known clients made this a high-profile case, and they were eager to handle it correctly.

The investigation started immediately after Lana called 911, and continued into the night. Sheski and some troopers, including Doug Zimmerman, a very young, new academy graduate, were now outside the Stone home, near the spot where Lana had seen the gardener.

Doug, of average height and build, with short blond hair, was on his hands and knees busily poking around the shrubbery, while Sheski was probing flower beds. Doug had recognized Sheski's Polish name and slight accent and, without thinking, proceeded to make the serious mistake of trying to kid his superior about it.

"Hey Polock," the exuberant trooper yelled excitedly to Sheski. "Come here, I have something you might be interested in."

The older statie bristled. He was proud of his heritage and had learned to take his part at times like this. Obviously, this green trooper had a lot to learn or he never would have used the P word.

The others knew Sheski and how he hated it with a passion when he was called a Polock, even in jest. A quiet collective gasp was heard from those nearby. As heads slowly turned to face the two men, they waited expectantly for the inevitable response.

Doug saw the expression on the older detective's face and realized he had done something wrong. His smile evaporated and his eyes were fearful. As a new graduate, he was still on probation and could not afford trouble.

Sheski slowly turned to see who had called to him. Spying the offending party, he pulled himself up to his full height and headed toward the inexperienced trooper with blood in his eye.

Doug stiffened and took a step back as he observed the much bigger, much annoyed Lieutenant approaching. Face slackened with apprehension, he steeled himself for an expected confrontation.

Sheski's body language told it all. Towering over the much smaller trooper, clenched fists at his sides, he got in the speechless man's face. Through gritted teeth, the older policeman made it clear that if he couldn't call him Lieutenant, Sheski, or Sir, he was NOT to address him at all. There was a long silence with Sheski standing his ground. Doug got the message. His face burned crimson and he mumbled an apology.

Sheski said nothing for a few minutes while his anger subsided. He looked around at the others, who pretended not to be paying attention.

Doug busied himself with tasks and remained quiet until the detective addressed him again.

"Now, what do you have for me, young man?" Sheski asked him. Although he was still annoyed, he was not one to hold a grudge. Besides, he was fairly certain the incident would not be repeated. Doug showed Sheski something long and heavy that he had spotted in the shrubbery. Sticking out from a bunch of Japanese Holly bushes was a four-foot garden pruner with wooden handles. It lay heavy end in first, as if someone had tossed it in haste. Small twigs were broken from the greenery where the weighty, vise-like jaws had smashed against them.

Taking a white cloth handkerchief out of his pocket, Doug reached down and picked it up. The metal end had unmistakable blood and flesh on it. Thinking of the dead woman just yards from him, Sheski said that he bet he knew who it came from. But, just to be sure, they carefully bagged it to be checked for a match with tissue from the corpse. Since they were doing their own forensics, results would be forthcoming a lot quicker than in the past.

From the garden, deep, undefined boot prints tracked through the rain-soaked ground and led to a small path behind the garage. They were lucky to still have some daylight available in which to view them.

The men thought the rain could start again any time now. The sky had ominous patches of black and the wind was picking up. Sheski was chilled. "November," he complained to no one in particular.

He pulled his overcoat closer to his neck and followed the damp path down about a hundred feet to a dirt road at the back of the property. He picked his way through the area, careful not to obliterate any evidence. From there, it appeared that whoever had made the tracks had gotten into a vehicle and left. Sheski called to the others to get castings of the footprints and tire tracks, although in their present rain-soaked condition, he doubted their usefulness.

"I hope we can get what we need here before the reporters and sightseers descend to contaminate the area," Sheski said, looking over at Doug. He knew that in a small town such as this, a lost cat was a big deal, so this murder was sure to draw attention as soon as word got out.

"Yes," added Doug. "We're gonna have to work fast." He knew the older detective was right, but would have agreed to almost anything to make amends for his earlier gaffe.

When the Sweetriver development was new, plans had called for the dirt road behind the Stones' home to be paved. The rolling acreage would then be cleared, underground utilities installed and the lots sold. Dr. and Mrs. Stone had put an end to that by purchasing the remaining heavily-wooded property. Rumor had it that they paid plenty for it, but the Stones could afford the additional cost. Besides, they didn't want the mature trees cut, preferring the pristine view. Included were about a dozen rare chestnut trees, some of the few in the state that had somehow survived a Pennsylvania blight in the early part of the 1900s. Also, they did not want anyone building on lots behind them.

The dirt road behind the home was the only other access route into the development but was not usually used because of its poor condition. Only utility men who served Sweetriver properties drove on it. Dr. Stone kept promising to close the road off but Rose had liked the idea that her hired help could get to their home without coming through the development. After all, she'd said, the men were usually soiled and drove old trucks.

"The gardener must have had his vehicle here and walked back to it when it was time to leave," Doug said.

"Maybe," Sheski replied. "Unless he's our guilty man. Didn't he hear what was happening inside the house and check it out? And where is he?"

Sheski and Doug reviewed notes of what they knew so far. Looking up, they saw Sergeant Cromley, who had been working on the interior crime scene, approaching them. Cromley gave the younger statie a "Boy did you goof" look, having heard about Doug's Polock remark. Doug got the message and turned away.

"According to the local police," Cromley said, "the Stones' gardener is named Barry Brown, and he drives an old Ford pickup. We were given a description of the vehicle and he said he'd fill you in later on what he knows about him."

"Thanks," Sheski replied. He assigned Doug the task of tracking the gardener down.

Back inside the Stones' home, Sheski started to address the questions that were swimming around in his head. Was this just a robbery, or was there another motive? If it was just a robbery, why was the victim so savagely attacked? Why not just knock her out and then take what was wanted? After all, she was a small person. Just about any man, or woman for that matter, could have cold-cocked her without too much trouble. Who was the person Mrs. Stone told Lana that she was expecting that day? Was anything else taken besides the jewelry? And where is Barry Brown? He had a lot of questions that needed answers.

Sheski was getting tired, but an investigation always succeeded in pumping him back up. He glanced over the shoulders of the other policemen, gleaning information from their conversations and notes.

One of the troopers, Jeff Morgan, an art aficionado, identified the blood-soaked shards near the body as the remains of an original 1925 Etling opalescent glass figurine. "Very expensive," he said, drawing the words out to emphasize their meaning. "Art Deco in style and probably made in Paris in the twenties," he went on. Jeff picked up the largest piece of the broken sculpture, the luminous orange torso of a woman enveloped in a pale blue-green diaphanous garment. Turning it over and over in his hand, he stated facetiously, "I'd kill for one of these."

Death was instantaneous, Sheski was told. Whoever

killed Rose knew what they were doing. The massive blow to the brain stem smashed the midbrain, pons and medulla into pulp. It happened so fast that the reticular formation had scant time to relay life-sustaining sensory information to any part of her body. Respiratory and cardiac functions ceased almost immediately. Those who loved her could take solace in knowing that she did not suffer.

There were no defensive wounds on Rose's hands. Her acrylic nails, painted dark red, were all intact, and there appeared to be no material beneath them. She hadn't had time to protect herself. The attack was sudden. She probably didn't even know what hit her. Why, then, did her assailant continue to pummel her? Sheski wondered.

Rose's expensive black suit now looked like a rag. Shards of dark silk were hanging off her body like party crepe paper. The amount of blood around was enough to ensure that whoever had killed her probably got some on himself. Sheski wondered whether the killer was the same person that Rose told Lana she was expecting. They would need an inventory of exactly what jewelry she had been wearing today. He was certain that Rose would only have expensive items. Things worth killing for.

While he was mulling over his questions and the evidence at hand, a statie approached and informed Sheski that Dr. Stone was at Stone Haven and had been told over the phone what had happened. When advised that a detective wanted to speak personally with him, the dead woman's widower insisted that Sheski come to his office for the interview. Sheski thanked the officer and began to mentally review what he would ask the surviving spouse. He would need someone with him, he reasoned. *It's now time to link up with Mike.*

Sheski stepped outside of the Stones' home to wait for his partner of many years, Lieutenant Mike James, a state police detective who was doing some background work at their office. He would be glad to see him.

In less than five minutes, his sidekick pulled in the driveway, got out, and spent a few minutes surveying the crime scene. Sheski waited at the car for him. When Mike came back out he gave a loud whistle and shook his head back and forth. Sheski opened the car door on the passenger's side, got in, and said, "Let's go see the doc."

On their way, Sheski filled his partner in on the details of the crime and they discussed their impending interview of the victim's husband.

Chapter Four

Sheski thanked his lucky stars that Lieutenant Mike James was on duty. He enjoyed the mental stimulation of interviewing suspects, but appreciated what Mike could bring to the job. Mike was smart, observant, and skilled with the public. He was known as a good family man to his wife Lillian and their two daughters. At average height, in his forties, with sandy brown hair and brown eyes, Detective James appeared kindly and maybe even naive to those who had not met him on the wrong side of the law. Appearances are deceiving. Mike was intelligent, wiry, and quick. His All American wrestling background at Bloomsburg University had gotten him out of more than one grapple with a punk who thought he could take the smaller lawman. Sheski often chuckled at the sight of an over-confident thug in a chicken-wing hold. He was glad

Mike was going with him to Dr. Stone's office at Stone Haven. He needed his friend's expertise for this one.

It was now getting dark, and driving through the wrought-iron gates of Stone Haven, formerly the Danville Medical Hospital, Sheski felt as if he were stepping back into time. Gray night skies and the facility itself had that effect on observers.

Danville Medical Hospital had been built for the area's residents in the 1880s by Andrew Ashman, a wealthy ironworks owner. He donated five acres a half-mile northwest of Danville, and oversaw construction of the hospital on a grassy knoll. On the lower end of the property, there was a pond that provided ice during the winter. When the water froze fourteen inches deep, blocks were cut and placed in sawdust-filled sheds until needed by the hospital.

The brick hospital campus was surrounded by beautiful lawns with a high, iron fence that had been produced at the Ashman Iron Mill in town. Building bricks for the hospital were fired at one of the local factories on Continental Boulevard in Danville. The faux marble fireplaces for heating were painted by Oliver Pratt, a Philadelphia artist admitted to the medical hospital in the 1890s.

The son of a wealthy Philadelphia physician, Oliver was sent to Danville by his horrified father upon the young man's conviction for murder in a much-publicized trial in the City of Brotherly Love. The city was not feeling very brotherly toward the artist after the facts of his heinous crimes were known. However, his influential physician father got the judge to rule that the young artist was insane and needed to be treated at the small psychiatric unit in the Danville Medical Hospital, which was financially supported by a Pratt family friend, Mr. Ashman. Pratt's father secreted his son out of the city under the cover of darkness, sending him on the 3 A.M. train to Danville to live out the remainder of his life there. Shortly after the killer's admission to the hospital, the judge retired and managed somehow to live very well on a modest pension.

Original florid hospital records and the pages of the *Philadelphia Inquirer* documented Oliver's obsession with little girls and his subsequent conviction for the murders of six blond, blue-eyed females between the ages of five and ten. All of the victims were found buried in shallow graves in a vacant lot behind Oliver's center-city studio, naked, their necks broken, with unmistakable traces of pigment on their tiny fingers and toes. The various colors of sky blue, ochre, and burnt sienna appeared to the observer as if indulgent mothers were obliging their daughter's budding feminine desire to polish their nails. Only Oliver knew what had transpired between the time these unfortunate tow-headed little girls met the congenial Mr. Pratt and the discovery of their bodies. The painter refused to disclose those details, citing an artist's privilege to his secrets. In his twisted psyche, he did not understand the public's rage at his rationale. In Oliver's mind, he was merely protecting himself from others stealing his techniques. The court-committed artist, still alert and agile, and painting each morning in his hospital studio, died suddenly in 1937 at the age of seventy-one.

The beautifully painted fireplaces and murals on the hospital walls give no hint of the painter's gruesome past. His style was unmistakable, and a large *P* in the left corner of his paintings, with a smiling child's face inside the loop, was Pratt's signature. It could be found on all of his artwork.

Danville Medical Hospital was one of the few public buildings to have electric lights in the nineteenth century. Thomas Edison was well into marketing a delivery system for his incandescent light bulb when the hospital's plans were being drawn. While in Sunbury, Danville's neighboring community, debuting for the first time anywhere the wiring of a city street, the inventor saw the hospital's blueprints. Upon completion of the three-wire electric lighting system installed at the City Hotel, Edison made plans to visit friends upstream in Danville.

The inventor came to town, staying at the Montour Hotel on Mill Street to personally oversee the ten horsepower dynamo-driven wiring of the new hospital. It was rumored that he spent most of his evenings cloistered in a second-floor hotel room, working on his moving pictures invention, barely stopping to sleep or bathe. Upon completion of the hospital's project, he would not visit the town again until arriving in the area in 1922 for the sesquicentennial celebration in Sunbury.

Danville Medical Hospital's staff cared for the needs

of Montour County citizens until 1932, when the hospital just couldn't survive those rough times of an economy in shambles. Mr. Ashman was pleased to be out from under the burden when it was eventually scaled down to accommodate only the twenty-six patients left in residence. Accepting no new admissions, the hospital continued providing care for each one until the last expired in 1939.

Wealthy Elizabeth Hastings Stone, attorney Louis Garfield Stone's wife and the mother of Dr. Lesley Stone, then purchased the property for a mere $25,000. She hadn't a clue what she was going to do with it, but bought it anyway. Mrs. Stone had no way of knowing that her acquisition would, many years later, become Stone Haven, a refuge for the mentally ill. She made the purchase because she adored the grounds and the architecture. She enjoyed spending her money.

Elizabeth was a highly respected philanthropist whose interests ranged from the local library that family friend Thomas Beaver had built for Danville citizens, to the high school her sons Lesley and Samuel attended. A religious woman, she also gave large sums of money to missionaries.

Stone Haven's Victorian effect was not lost on Sheski. Knowing it was a center for the mentally ill, he imagined a multitude of bizarre crazies drooling and relieving themselves on the tile and parquet flooring. His imaginings were far from the reality of present-day life there.

At any given time, only ten to twenty private-paying clients from America's wealthiest families find respite on the first floor of the building. They are meticulously cared for and rarely seen by outsiders.

Stone Haven's caseload not in residence arrives under a cloak of privacy at conveniently scheduled times of the day for sessions with psychiatrists Dr. Lesley Stone or Dr. Richard Burns. Clients also receive services from a social worker, dietician, nurse, and other professionals hired to meet the patient's individual needs.

Dr. Stone founded the private hospital for the east coast's wealthy in 1976, in memory of his deceased brother Samuel. According to the local police report to Sheski, both Lesley and Samuel had inherited the property in July 1968 from their mother. Attorney Louis Stone, their father, had already been dead for two years from a heart attack.

Sheski read in the police background report that Lesley and Samuel's mother's untimely death occurred in a car accident on the convoluted back road to Catawissa while on her way to an appointment with her interior decorator. Long black skid marks at the accident scene led officers to conclude that Elizabeth Stone had braked and swerved to avoid hitting someone or something that had wandered onto the black macadam road. With no guardrails to prevent what happened next, the attractive, wealthy, middle-aged woman perished as her Rolls Royce impacted on the railroad tracks below. She died at the scene.

The hospital property became Lesley's exactly one year later when his bachelor brother Samuel, a manic-depressive taking the newly-introduced Lithium, accidentally drowned. He reportedly had wandered naked down Ferry Street during a late-night manic episode and walked into the Susquehanna River, murky from recent upriver rainfall. Samuel was often noncompliant with his med regimen, resulting in some brushes with the law. This time there were dire consequences when his blood level dipped below the narrow range of therapeutic efficacy. His drowning left Lesley as the sole heir to the immense Stone family fortune. Sheski reflected on the many disastrous happenings in Dr. Stone's family.

Stone Haven bears no resemblance to early psychiatric hospitals where the patients spent their time wailing or responding to unseen stimuli and receiving more primitive treatments. This facility takes pride in providing, for an undisclosed fee, well-staffed private treatment for those who can afford it. Inpatient clients stay in immaculate individual small apartments equipped with antique furniture, high-tech entertainment equipment, and, when permitted, kitchenettes. Only the best of medical and psychiatric care, therapies, and dining options are provided. Rumor has it that a few wives and behavior-problem offspring of statesmen, performers, and powerful men are in residence. They are mentally ill, depressed, or have eating disorders or compulsions, and are said to be spending their lives carefully and expensively tucked away in Stone Haven suites. Staff persons are forbidden to discuss their clients' identities, so the rumors go unsubstantiated. They know that they would face immediate dismissal from their positions should an indiscretion occur. Anonymity and excellent care have kept the census up and a long waiting list intact.

Sheski pulled into a visitor's parking place, turned off the engine, took a deep breath, and said to Mike, "Let's get this over with." Their observant eyes scanned the grounds as they walked through the doors and crossed the tiled floors. Approaching the receptionist's desk, the lawmen flashed badges and identified themselves. Sheski asked the receptionist for directions to Dr. Stone's office.

"Are you two carrying any weapons?" Sarah, the receptionist/secretary queried. "We don't permit weapons inside Stone Haven, not even on policemen. Policy, you know."

Sheski observed Sarah as she talked. She was attractive with an average build and looked to be in her late twenties.

Sarah expected opposition to relinquishing their weapons. She was accustomed to resistance from policemen when it came to the issue of their firearms, and braced herself for the refusal. None was forthcoming.

The two men were prepared for this. Stone Haven had a reputation known to lawmen when it came to weapons. They rarely had to come here, but on those occasions it was expected that John Deadly, Stone Haven's security man, would confiscate whatever firearms they were carrying.

Sarah paged John, who arrived quickly. Because of his name, John Deadly was something of a joke for those who had contact with him in security matters. The name Deadly did not seem to suit the diminutive

5'6" man. However, after just minutes in his presence, a person's initial view took a 180-degree turn. John Deadly, a retired army veteran, backed down from no one. His steely gaze, deep voice, and firm adherence to security procedures were unshakable.

His only redeeming quality that acquaintances had discovered was a love of gardening and art. Upon engaging him in conversation regarding those topics, one would find that he became uncharacteristically obliging and animated.

Deadly was wearing a blue uniform with a gold lettered shield above the left breast pocket. His gray hair fell just below the top of his ears and was crowned by a blue tam-'o-shanter, which was cocked to the right side of his head. A thick ring of keys of all shapes and sizes dangled noisily on his right groin area from a short chain attached to a thick black belt. In his early sixties, he was still quick, and wasted no time in relieving the two officers of their standard issue .40-caliber Glocks. After the weapons were locked inside the hospital vault, Deadly escorted the men to an elevator leading to Dr. Stone's second-floor office.

Walking in front of the security man, both troopers were aware that he was watching them closely. Their attempts to engage him in conversation brought nothing more than a curt answer. Apparently he was not interested in small talk. At least not with them. They rode the elevator silently to the second floor.

As they exited and went the short distance to Dr. Stone's office door, their escort broke his silence and grunted, "What brings State Police detectives here to

Stone Haven? We don't see much of you guys. Is there
a security issue I should be aware of?"

Deadly was eyeing them suspiciously while he waited for their reply.

"We need to talk with Dr. Stone at this time," Sheski
stated evenly. "If you're to be included in our scope of
interviews, we will certainly be getting back to you."

From the petulant look on Deadly's face, he did not
appreciate being left out of the loop. He replied uncon-
vincingly, "I'll help in any way I can."

Sheski knocked on the wood door, and the three men
waited for the psychiatrist.

Dr. Lesley Stone greeted the troopers at his office
entrance and invited them in with firm handshakes,
flashing his security man a wary look that neither officer could interpret. Deadly looked back and then
retreated down the hall.

Sheski displayed his badge, offered the psychiatrist
their condolences, and waited for the shaken man to
compose himself. He was glad someone had already
phoned with the bad news.

"Dr. Stone, we need to ask you some questions,"
Sheski began, hoping he could soon take a seat. It was
now 6:15 P.M. and he was tired from the demands of his
job. At the age of fifty-four, Sheski was burning out and
he knew it. He was showing all the signs. *Once this
case is over,* he thought, *I'm gonna take a long vacation
to somewhere the sun always shines, and far enough
away that if people are murdered, I won't have to get
involved.*

The psychiatrist stood near a chair behind his desk,

dabbed at his eyes with a monogrammed handkerchief, and replied in a broken voice, "Of course I'll try to help all I can. I want to find the bastard who did this to Rose. Oh, God," he said mournfully, "she was so lovely, so perfect. There isn't another like her. She had everything a woman could want."

Dr. Stone began to slow his speech. "I loved her so much."

He slowly lowered his tall frame into the leather desk chair and covered his eyes with his hands. Dressed in an expensive dark suit, and dark shirt and tie, he was what men and women alike would call a good-looking man. Educated at Harvard, he had both a medical degree and an MBA. The masters degree, he correctly thought, would help him with Stone Haven's business demands.

Sheski waited a few minutes for the doc to compose himself. He and Mike kept their eyes on him. They didn't get this far up the state police ladder by not being observant. Their subject made no sound. He just sat there, head in hands. So they waited.

Sheski leaned against a mahogany sideboard that held a crystal decanter with eight small glasses, a bronze replica of the Medici horse, and some old hospital memorabilia in a locked, glass case. He shifted his gaze from the doctor and leaned over to view the artifacts that were identified by neatly-typed cards glued beneath each object. Once-tortuous trephining tools, three white porcelain feeding cups with *Danville Medical Hospital* hand-painted in gold leaf on the front, and a well-worn, eight-by-ten, leather-bound book completed the collection. The writing on the kid leather cover was illegible but its typed card identified it as the *Journal of Oliver Pratt.* Sheski raised an eyebrow and thought that it looked interesting.

Above the sideboard, placed side by side, were two beautifully painted scenes of the Susquehanna river at the turn of the century. They were showcased in massive ornate gold frames. Sheski leaned closer and squinted to read the painter's signature. A single *P* with a little girl's face painted in the loop was discernible in the left lower corner of each picture. He nudged Mike to take a look, which he did. They then stood silently in front of Dr. Stone's desk and waited. Waiting quietly during an interrogation was an art, and, despite fatigue, Sheski was a master.

The statie looked further around the office. Obviously the doc had done well for himself. Large picture windows overlooked a small bar and sideboard. Two couches and a fireplace provided a cozy nook for restful thought. Behind the massive desk, a filled bookcase wound around the room. It looked comfortable, yet practical.

Dr. Stone lifted his head and asked in a quiet voice, "What do you want to know?"

Sheski went first. "Well, for starters, where were you today between the hours of three P.M. and now?"

The coroner had estimated the time of death to be about 4:10 P.M., shortly before Lana arrived at the Stones' residence. *Somebody had a lot of nerve murdering this woman in broad daylight,* thought Sheski. *And psychiatrists usually have a lot of nerve.* Sheski and Mike both knew that the spouse is always the main suspect at the beginning of a murder case. This one was no different. The doc had better have a good alibi.

Dr. Stone slowly opened his schedule book and reviewed the day's planned events. He ran his finger down the page and said quietly, "Please sit down while I clear my head." Both officers thankfully seated themselves on an overstuffed couch and were surprised by its comfort.

"I was having a private session with one of my clients," Dr. Stone went on. "I don't need to remind either of you that any patient's name is privileged information, but you can verify my story with my secretary."

Sheski made a mental note to do just that.

"Go on."

"Well, the session began at three-thirty and continued for two hours. My client was scheduled for just a one-hour session, but we were making progress, so I permitted it to go longer than planned. My next client wasn't scheduled until now, so I had plenty of time."

The doctor's face changed as he realized he had forgotten something. "Oh, excuse me, I must tell Sarah to cancel my six-thirty appointment." He hurriedly picked up his phone and made a call.

The troopers waited patiently while Dr. Stone informed Sarah of the reason for the police visit, and asked her to make the cancellation. "Oh, yes," he said as an afterthought, "please notify Dr. Burns of Rose's death, too."

Sarah must have told him the client was standing there waiting because the doctor became frustrated, and asked her to please handle the matter. He quickly placed the receiver on its base. Stone took a few moments to regain his composure and, leaning back on his chair, stared blankly at the detectives, waiting for their next question.

Sheski had been thinking about the fees that the wealthy families were being charged for Stone Haven services. He didn't know what the cost was, but was sure it was more than his salary. He grimaced, thinking how a policeman puts his life on the line every day for five figures a year while others, whose only peril is awaiting the country club's approval to join, rake in the kind of dough required to live life at its best.

It was at that moment that Dr. Stone's clear blue eyes enlarged, his mouth dropped open and he rose out of his chair, holding onto the desktop with white knuckles. "Oh, no," he said in a low voice, touching his right hand to his forehead, "has anyone told Karen yet?" He was referring to his and Rose's only child. He stared back and forth from one detective to the other and rapidly repeated his question.

Sheski had been wondering why the doc was taking so long to think of her.

"She will need me to be with her when she's told," the doctor said firmly. "Karen and her mother have not been very close these past months, and this will be a terrible shock to her."

"We have someone trying to locate your daughter now. As soon as Karen is found, I'll be paged and we'll go talk to her. You're welcome to come along with us." He paused and then, looking Lesley directly in the eyes, asked, "Why were your wife and daughter estranged?"

Dr. Stone's handsome face showed signs of strain as he remembered the difficulties they had with Karen. "She's thirty years old now. It's hard to believe that our little girl is grown and an accomplished artist." He sighed and looked away from the detectives before continuing his story.

"Raised in a family of wealth, our daughter was accustomed to having anything and everything that she wanted," he explained. "She never took no for an answer, although 'no' was something she rarely heard." He frowned at that disclosure. "Whenever we tried to set limits, it led to rebellion and tantrums. She would stay out all night or refuse to talk to us until we caved in." He went on to explain unapologetically, "which we usually did."

The psychiatrist continued by explaining that they lavished expensive clothing and presents on their daughter from the time that she was born. "We knew," Lesley said quietly, "that Karen would be our only child. We were told the morning after our daughter's birth that, due to delivery complications, Rose could never conceive again. She took the news hard and plunged into a six-month postpartum depression. So deeply did she internalize her anger and sadness that she crawled into her bed and stayed there for the first two months of Karen's life, only getting up to use the adjoining powder room to take care of her personal needs."

How fortunate for her to have a live-in psychiatrist, thought Sheski.

As if reading his mind, Dr. Stone said, "Rose refused

psychiatric therapy, but accepted an antidepressant. She began to improve and, four weeks later, got out of bed and told me that she was headed to the Pocono mountains in northeastern Pennsylvania. She returned renewed from the exclusive Lincoln Spa north of Scranton, and began caring for Karen, who was already learning to sit up unaided."

Sheski thought there must have been scant opportunity for the young mother and infant daughter to bond.

"It was Karen's birthday when I presented Rose with the Darling Diamond ring," the doctor explained. "I was ecstatic about the birth, so I also had a matching one-carat ring made for Karen. Both were hand-crafted one-of-a-kinds by Hiram Goldblum, a New York City specialty goldsmith." Lesley enjoyed talking about his possessions and, momentarily pushing aside the reason for the interview, became engaging.

"There are none like it anywhere. The one-carat stone was purchased on diamond row when I was in Manhattan. The nine-carat was part of an inheritance from my mother."

The psychiatrist went on to proudly explain that his daughter received her ring on her tenth birthday, when other birthday girls her age were getting dolls.

"Karen was the only student in grade school with her own diamond ring," he boasted. He told of how she regularly wore it to classes, making the faculty very nervous. When Karen's teacher approached her parents with the suggestion that, for safety's sake, the little girl not wear the ring to school, Rose and Dr. Stone threw their weight around and the suggestion was reluctantly withdrawn.

Sheski's face did not betray the sick feeling he had about a kid sporting an expensive piece of jewelry at school. *No wonder she gave them such a bad time,* he thought, *she had no boundaries placed on her.*

"Whoever stole my ring will have to take great care where they sell it," Dr. Stone said harshly. "The diamond has quite a provenance and is well known in the jewelry circles. It will be instantly recognized."

He added, "It is priceless, and I want it back."

"What was the reason for the estrangement?" Sheski asked again. From the way the doctor avoided his question the first time, he got the impression that the man didn't really want to tell him.

Doctor Stone chewed on his lower lip, picked up his pen, tapped it nervously on the rosewood desk, and said matter-of-factly, "I might as well tell you . . . it's no secret, really."

The lawmen sensed anger and pain as events of the Valentine's Day confrontation at their home were recalled.

"Rose and I were expecting Karen and a friend for dinner at eight o'clock. We were both happy to be seeing her since she had telephoned us to say that she would be bringing a very special date along with her, someone whom she wanted us to meet. We discussed who this could be, hoping that our daughter had finally found a steady boyfriend, perhaps even a serious relationship. Not that Karen had trouble getting dates," Lesley was quick to explain. "She's pretty, and intelligent, too. She just went from one man to another, wearing them down with her incessant demands. Karen always has to have her way, you see. I just don't understand how she got like that." He looked at the detectives, who nodded back but hid their lack of surprise at this last statement.

"When her present boyfriend wouldn't do what she wanted, she moved on to another, with no regrets. If it ever bothered her, you wouldn't know it." Lesley shook his head back and forth as he thought about Karen's need to be controlling.

"I was busy in the kitchen preparing del monicos and salads when I heard Karen's car pull up the lane. Rose had prepared the dining room with our best linen and china for what we hoped was a special occasion. She could really set a table, and went all out."

The troopers listened closely as he went on to tell the story. The gold tableware was in use and fresh pink roses were in a crystal vase on the table. Twelve-inch pink tapers finished off the effect. Rose opened the door for the couple after the bell rang and immediately called for Lesley to join them in the living room.

Lesley noticed tension in his wife's voice, thought something might be wrong, and put the steaks back into the refrigerator. The sight of Karen with an attractive black man took him by surprise. Neither he nor Rose were prepared for what followed.

Karen informed the two of them that her date, Jess Walter, had asked her to marry him and that she had accepted. She had met him at one of her art classes at Bucknell University, where Jess was an Art History professor. They had been secretly dating for six months. Happiness shone on the faces of the newly-engaged couple as Karen waved a large solitaire in the air in front of her. She then leaned over to give Jess's arm a squeeze, beaming up at him.

Lesley's face was dark with anger. "Rose recoiled in horror. She couldn't believe what she was hearing and seeing, and loudly said so."

"What are you thinking?" Rose had screamed at the couple. "What will our friends think, Karen?" She exploded. "You come from a prestigious family, you can do better than this. You know how people in a small town can be. You will never be accepted here; there will be gossip when this gets out." Rose then turned to her husband, her face flushed with anger, her body shaking. "Say something, Lesley—for God's sake, don't just stand there."

Lesley told the police officers that he could barely speak. His daughter was obviously very happy, but she couldn't have given this relationship much thought, or reflected on what this could mean to her and her family. "Lord knows we aren't prejudiced, but this will never work," he remembered telling the two of them.

According to the doctor, Jess silently listened while his fiancée's parents presented all the reasons why the relationship should end and the nuptials should not take place. He recognized that this was not the time for a showdown and stated that he loved their daughter very much and was sorry that they felt the way that they did. With dignity and reserve, he then turned to make his exit.

Karen glared at her parents, told them they were bigoted and hadn't even given Jess a chance, then followed him out the door. The whole scene hadn't taken more than ten minutes.

As the couple was making their way down the walk, Rose opened the door and flung the final insult their way. "You'll never get another dime from us, Karen, as long as that . . . that man is in your life. If you marry him, everything we have will go somewhere else, anywhere but to you."

Karen slowly turned, eyes flashing, still holding Jess's hand. Choosing her words carefully, she made her own position clear. "I don't need your money," she rasped through clenched teeth. "My work is providing me with a very good living. And Mother," she said insultingly, "Jess has given me love. Something I was sadly missing!"

Walking down the glass-imbedded sidewalk, with tears in her eyes, Karen looked back and slung the final arrow. "Don't bother calling me until you two have changed your minds," she said. They knew she meant it.

Dr. Stone described how, from that time forward, the relationship with their daughter was changed. They didn't know where she spent her time, nor with whom. Karen and her parents hadn't seen nor spoken to each other since. That was almost nine months ago. It was now November and the holidays were approaching with no contact made. The Stones blamed the fiancé for the schism, and never forgave him. Time only made it worse as the parents agonized over their daughter's stubbornness and prayed that she would come to her senses.

It was at this point in Dr. Stone's story that Sheski's pager vibrated against his right hip. The detective made his apologies as he reached down to read the message.

"May I use your phone?" he asked.

Dr. Stone nodded.

Sheski dialed his office number, wrote something down on a pad, and glancing at the doctor, said, "They've located Karen. She's in her studio behind her home. Lieutenant Anderson told her to expect us soon."

The psychiatrist stated that they should go on out and he would meet them at their car in a few minutes. From there, they could follow him to his daughter's home.

The officers started toward the office door. Before touching the doorknob, Sheski turned to the doctor and said carefully, "Oh, yes. I'll need a complete list of the jewelry your wife was wearing today, and we still have some questions about your gardener."

"Of course," he replied.

The two men walked toward the elevator and got in, and Mike pushed the button for the first floor. They murmured back and forth and headed to the large front doors. Walking past the receptionist's desk, they saw Sarah speaking to John Deadly.

"Doctor Stone wants to speak to you immediately," they heard her say to the security man. Deadly frowned and hurriedly turned, almost bumping into Mike.

"Sorry," he said absently, and hurried off in the direction of the elevator.

As they looked at him, then back at Sarah, they noticed several of the female staff standing around, whispering. Somber faces turned to watch the detectives. *They must have all heard the news,* Sheski thought.

Sarah, the boldest of the three, stepped forward to intercept the officers at the massive front doors. "We just heard about Rose," she began. "How is Dr. Stone taking it?"

"He seems pretty shaken," Mike offered. "But I think he'll be alright."

"Well, I can't say that any of us here are too upset. Rose didn't have many friends. She was snobby from the first day we met her, waving that big gaudy diamond back and forth all the time. The few times that she came here, she walked past my desk straight to her husband's office without a word to anyone."

Sarah's face was flushed as she went on, and she looked at them as if expecting a comment. When none was forthcoming, she went on. "Rose made a lot of enemies in this town."

Sheski was taken aback by her harsh commentary. He knew that people often blurt out information to police officers in the heat of the moment, and later regret it. He believed this was one of those times.

"I'll be calling to set up an appointment to talk with you . . . on the record," he said professionally.

Sarah composed herself and looked over the handsome detective from head to toe.

"I'll be looking forward to it," she said with a smile. With that, she rejoined the others at her desk.

When they had left the building and were in their car out of others' hearing range, Mike whistled loudly. "Wow. It looks like Mrs. Rose Stone didn't have any friends there. And what about the daughter and her boyfriend?"

Before Sheski could answer, Dr. Stone pulled up in his black Mercedes and waved for them to follow him. As they exited the Stone Haven parking lot, a large white limousine with tinted windows pulled in and parked close to the front door. The officers strained to see who would get out of one of its six doors, but no one emerged until their car was out of viewing distance.

Chapter Five

Oliver Pratt lowered himself down onto his cot and stared at the high, cracked ceiling. He was on the top floor of the hospital, tucked under one of the gables of the west wing of the psychiatric unit, and it was so hot up there. The windows had iron bars over them so he was able to put the sash up about four inches for some fresh air. He stuck his face against the peeling paint and sucked in air. The heat began to lull him into a dreamy state, one in which he often permitted himself to be drawn. It made his life bearable, reliving those earlier years in Philadelphia when he was a bright young painter still living with his father, the respectable Dr. Pratt. Instead of being sent out like some criminal to an insignificant backwoods village hospital, he should be enjoying the good life in Philly, he thought.

A smile slowly lifted the corners of his lined mouth as he recalled what he considered to be the most fun of his existence. In captivity or out, he had never experienced more pleasure. He didn't want to think about how difficult it was for him now to not be able to exercise his passion.

To ease this discomfort, he drifted back to those earlier years. He found it interesting how easy it was to gain the trust of the beautiful little girls. He liked them beautiful and very, very young. Less than ten years old. And they liked him. At least at first. To get them to open up and talk, he spoke softly to them about whatever it was he thought would catch their attention. If they were holding a doll, he tenderly touched the doll first and told its owner how pretty it was. If they had a storybook, he quietly and sincerely offered to read it to them. And did so. It came so easily to him.

He often spent days alone in his studio behind his father's home, engrossed in his painting, so when he was able to isolate one of his lovely young victims, that was where he took them. A meticulously lettered NO ADMITTANCE, ARTIST AT WORK sign hanging on the outside of his door assured his privacy while he taught the child about oils and pigments, and much, much, more.

The children's bodies were eventually found when a pack of wild dogs following a strong and familiar scent dug open one of the shallow graves. To the horror of those who witnessed the obscene display, the sweet, lifeless little girls, now covered in dirt and grime, looked like grisly dolls. Their dainty fingers and toes still held scant traces of bright-colored paint on the nails. It took the police a long time to piece all of the evidence together and finally figure out that the eccentric young artist who spent so much time alone painting in his studio was the monster who preyed on these little ones.

Oliver mentally relived every moment of the time spent with each of his little sweethearts. His rapid breathing gradually became shallow and regular as he happily drifted off to sleep with visions of happier times playing over and over in his dreams.

Chapter Six

On their way to Karen's home, the detectives discussed what they knew so far on this case. Sheski had something else on his mind, too. He was replaying his conversation with the woman who had found Rose's body. What if he had misjudged her, and she had something to do with it? It was a troubling question. He had no reason to suspect her, but he liked her and needed reassurance she was everything he thought she was.

The men continued their discussion as they followed the Mercedes to the farmette that Karen Stone called home. They talked about Jess Walter, Karen's fiancé, and his importance in their investigation. In the darkness, they made a turn down her dirt lane. The house was a far cry from the luxurious mansion at Sweetriver, but it was homey and welcoming. When they got closer, both studied the moderate-sized

nineteenth-century farmhouse with an adjoining out–
kitchen, perched on a knoll of gently rolling farmland.
Against the November sunset, a stand of yellow pines
framed the southern exposure of the white clapboard
dwelling. Flower gardens hemmed in by mountain
stone held promises of irises, daffodils, and cosmos to
come in the spring. Birdbaths and tiny water ponds
dotted the landscape. On the west side of the home, a
gently flowing brook fed by an artesian well from an
upper copse of trees made its way into a small wooded
area.

An artist's home, Sheski thought.

The two cars slowly snaked their way down the lane,
past a red banked barn and two empty corn cribs.

Karen had already received a call from an officer at
the State Police barracks, so she knew they were coming . . . and why. She initially was in shock, walking
unseeing and unfeeling from room to room, twisting a
small diamond pinky ring repeatedly around her finger.
Now, she was peering anxiously through the sheer curtains of a front room window. The kindly state policeman on the phone had told Karen that her mother was
found dead at home, apparently murdered, and that
Lieutenants Sheski and James would be there shortly.
He broke it to her as gently as one could tell such grisly news over the telephone.

Karen's lover, Jess, was not at the farm. He had
explained to her earlier his intentions of staying in his
office most of the day to work. She called to tell him
what had happened, but he didn't answer. Initially, in

her nervousness, she was having difficulty pushing the correct numbers and figured she had dialed the wrong number. She tried calling the campus operator, who said Professor Walter had signed out after an earlier meeting and hadn't been seen since.

Karen then called the janitor in Jess's building and insisted that he check the space where her fiancé had parked his black sport utility vehicle. He did as she asked, and called right back to tell her that it wasn't there. She hung up on him without a thank-you, and thoughts frantically raced through her mind. *Where is he? He said he'd be in his office. Maybe the janitor made a mistake.* She tried Jess's office again with no success.

The call from the state policeman played over and over in her mind. He wouldn't answer any of her questions despite her insistence on knowing the details. Old habits are hard to break and Karen found herself bullying the statie. Ignoring his kindness, Karen demanded to know his name and that of his superior. She would see to it that he was called on the carpet for not giving her what she wanted. Who did he think he was? She wasn't just any ordinary citizen, she was a well-known artist and the daughter of a wealthy family. Angry and upset, she was ready for the lieutenants.

Dr. Stone pulled into a parking space, got out of his Mercedes, and approached the policemen at the side of their car.

Sheski and Mike were reaching for the door handles when the radio squawked. It was Doug. He had news about the gardener, Barry Brown. Sheski briskly turned his back to the others, walked away from the cars and dialed Doug on his car phone.

Not wanting the victim's spouse to overhear private police business, Mike quickly took him aside and asked him a few more questions. The two of them then stood at the back of the Mercedes and waited for Sheski to finish.

Doug recounted how he had tried to find the gardener, with no luck. He put out an all points bulletin in the hopes that someone would come across him or his truck. If Barry tried to leave the area, they wanted the police ready to pick him up.

Doug said he had learned quite a bit about the gardener from Jacob Zimmerman, the owner of Zimmerman's Gardening. Jacob had given him a thorough description and the background of the worker who was assigned to Dr. and Mrs. Lesley Stone's property.

Barry was referred to Zimmerman's Gardening by Dr. Richard Burns when the psychiatrist couldn't find other employment for his former patient. The doctor believed the borderline menally retarded, with a primary diagnosis of Explosive Behavior Disorder, was now well-controlled through medication and therapy and could make a positive contribution to the community. Besides, Barry was the grandson of the owner of a large real estate business who was a friend of the Burnses.

Prior to the Stone Haven psychiatrists' getting him stabilized on a combination of psychotropic drugs, Barry had given his family much to worry about. There had been several occasions when he was housed in the Montour County jail for assault and battery. The family had a pending lawsuit from an incident a few years back when, in an apparent rage at a local bar, Barry had pummeled a much younger, much stronger man over a disagreement. Weeks later, after the man was released from the hospital, he had initiated a lawsuit against Barry Brown's family for not doing something about this dangerous relative. That's when Barry ended up in Stone Haven's care and Dr. Burns stepped in. Since he'd begun working for Zimmerman's, there had been no further incidents. Although he was not outgoing, Barry was the best gardener that Jacob had.

Jacob told Doug that Barry drove an old red Ford pickup, battered from years of hauling tools and supplies. The gardener used it to access Sweetriver via a dirt road behind the Stones' home.

Barry was plain-looking, with brown hair, brown eyes and a hooded gaze. He spoke very little, giving minimal eye contact from dull, unexpressive features. He was a small man, and, when he took his meds, posed no problem. An excellent worker, he was meticulous about his job. The Stones' property attested to that. Barry handled the grounds without assistance, and satisfied even the fussy Rose Stone.

When Doug recounted the details of the murder, Jacob was unconvinced of Barry's involvement. "It doesn't fit," he had said. "Barry's only interested in his work these days. Besides, he barely even speaks to anyone anymore. No, they were wrong," the gardener's boss had told him. "Barry's a changed man and couldn't have done that." The police were unconvinced.

Chapter Seven

While Sheski and Mike were busy interviewing Dr. Stone and his daughter, Doug went in search of Barry, the gardener. The trooper drove to the three-room shotgun cottage that Barry rented near the now abandoned armory at the end of West Mahoning Street in Danville. If he was hiding out there, Doug wanted to get to him before he was involved in more violence.

It was dark when Doug arrived, making the small home, sitting back from the road, appear spooky to the young trooper. He stepped onto the front porch and peered through the door window. He reached for the white glass doorknob and, finding it unlocked, pushed it open, and called loudly for Barry to come out. The statie waited for a reply. Receiving none, he called out again and then slowly stepped inside. He reached around the doorway and groped the wall for a light switch.

The ceiling light came on, casting a muted yellow glow around the small cottage. Doug cautiously moved from one room directly into the other. There was no sign of the occupant. Used furniture that Barry had purchased at the Salvation Army was polished and carefully arranged in each of the three small rooms. Doug shuffled along an outside wall of what appeared to be the main sitting room, pausing to rest his hand on a dark Mission-style end table. The cottage interior was eerily neat and clean and gave no clue to its inhabitant's whereabouts.

Doug's heart was pounding. He pulled his gun from its holster near his right ribcage and continued slowly through each of the three rooms, to the back door, and out into the yard. He warily stepped onto the brick sidewalk in the tiny grassy area, looking back and forth for signs of the gardener. Several stray cats, waiting at dishes that had been placed near the back of the house, screeched and scattered out of sight, frightening the policeman. Sweat beads rolled down his fair skin and onto his dark uniform. *The home's occupant had obviously been feeding quite a few of the strays regularly, judging from the eight or ten empty aluminum pie plates in view,* Doug thought. Licked clean, they didn't look like food had been placed on them recently. The young statie walked the outside perimeter of the neatly-kept house, detecting nothing of interest. He looked for Barry's truck, but it was nowhere in sight. Hearing Mahoning Creek gurgling nearby, he gazed in its direction through the shadowy woods behind the cottage and decided to look no further.

Relaxing from having found the property empty, and eager to stay in Sheski's good graces, Doug immediately telephoned the lieutenant to keep him posted.

Chapter Eight

Sheski listened closely as Doug reported in, turned to observe Mike keeping Dr. Stone occupied, and then told Doug to continue his search. Frowning, Sheski made his way back to the others.

"Oh, by the way," the doctor said to Sheski when he got within hearing distance, "I made up a list for you of the jewelry that Rose was wearing today." He showed the lieutenant a paper with hastily-scribbled words on it. "I'll have it typed and faxed to your office by tonight." Sheski thanked him for responding so quickly to his request.

The trio stepped up to the front door of Karen Stone's farmhouse and knocked. Her father was a few steps behind the state troopers.

Opening the door was an attractive young woman, obviously distraught, but composed enough to invite them in. She eyed her father, who immediately reached out to hug his daughter. With her arms at her sides, she let him embrace her and tell her how sorry he was. Karen started to cry and said nothing to him. She soon pulled away and motioned for them to sit down on an expensive-looking yellow sofa. Karen remained standing, anxiously pacing back and forth.

Sheski and Mike sat on the couch while Dr. Stone lowered himself into a nearby cherry rocker. The home was decorated in Early American antiques with plenty of chintz and soft cushions to make it cozy and comfortable.

"I'm Lieutenant Thomas Sheski and this is my partner, Lieutenant Mike James," Sheski said, motioning toward his partner. "We're sorry about your mother."

Mike extended his hand to Karen, murmuring his condolences. The young woman shook his hand.

She had regained control of her emotions enough to ask what she needed to know about her mother's death.

"Do you know who killed my mother?" Karen asked. Without waiting for an answer, she said, "I can't imagine how they got into the gated community without being seen. Unless they came in by that back road. I told you to get that road closed off," she said, turning to her father.

He looked uncomfortable but did not reply.

Her face and voice softened as she then asked how the murder happened.

Mike began to work the magic for which he was known by his peers. He calmly, gently, and with great care told Karen what details he could of her mother's murder. Leaning forward toward the young woman, he looked her in the eyes and his face presented an empathetic, understanding expression. His hands were relaxed on his legs and he occasionally provided her with opportunities to ask questions.

Mike left out critical privileged information and some of the gruesome details. Until the murderer was brought to justice, the police could not reveal everything.

Karen listened silently, her face belying her inner pain as the story was told. Skillfully, Mike walked her through the crime scene. How the body was discovered, the APB for Barry Brown, and the missing jewelry. It was at this point that Sheski saw her fingering an exquisite one-carat diamond on her right pinky finger.

Noticing the lieutenant's glance at her ring, Karen held it out for him to see. Tears were streaming down her face.

"This is an exact replica of my mother's stolen diamond. Father gave Mother hers when I was born. On my tenth birthday he presented me with this."

The two policemen admired the flawless stone set in platinum. Neither could fathom a ten-year-old receiving such an expensive gift. Neither lived in the same world as the Stones.

"Miss Stone," Sheski began.

"Call me Karen, please," she said.

"Karen, I have some questions that I must ask you. Please don't be offended; we must ask these of everyone close to your mother."

"I understand." Her misty eyes were downcast.

"Where were you today between the hours of three and five P.M.?"

Dr. Stone got up off his chair and said firmly, "She doesn't have to answer anything. What do you mean asking her that kind of a question at a time like this? Can't you see how upset she is? Karen, don't say anything until I get Jerry here."

Both staties knew Jerry Smithson, the Stones' family attorney, from past cases. He was a hard-nosed, capable lawyer but could quickly become annoying. He was always trying to drum up business wherever he was. In the grocery store, on the street corner, wherever, it didn't matter to him. Everyone was a potential client.

Karen spoke up. "Father, I can take care of myself. I have nothing to hide. Now, please," she said pleadingly, "wait out back in my studio while we finish this interview."

"I will not. You can't order me around. I'm your father," he said. Dr. Stone looked concerned as he added, "You don't know what they might ask you without Jerry present. You might say something that they could use against you later."

"I have nothing to hide," Karen replied. "Wait quietly in the studio while I talk with these men, or just go home."

Unwilling to leave at this point, Dr. Stone shot the troopers a frown. He went down a hallway to a room in the back of the house and they heard the studio door bang shut before they resumed their questioning.

Sheski rephrased the original question. "Can you tell me about your afternoon?"

"I was here working in my studio." She motioned to

the back room. "I have an art show coming up in the spring and I was preparing for it."

Sheski then told her that his colleagues had tried to contact her by telephone right after the body was discovered, but got no answer.

"I didn't hear the phone. When I'm concentrating on a project, I turn the ringer off so I won't be interrupted."

"Can anyone vouch for your presence here? How about your fiancé, Jess Walter? Your father told us about him."

"I'll just bet he did," Karen spat out. "Did he tell you about their shame? How I embarrassed them by getting involved with a black man? The bigots." She began to get intense, causing Sheski concern that Dr. Stone would hear her. Karen recounted her version of what happened on Valentine's Day, the last time she had been in her parents' home.

"You see, this is a small town we live in. And there are still a few people in our community with small minds. That includes my parents. When they saw who I brought to meet them that evening, they threw us out!" she exclaimed. "And for the first time in my life, my mother raised a hand to me. She slapped me hard across the face when I told them I had no intention of leaving Jess. I couldn't believe it! She slapped me! Did he tell you that?" she said, looking in the direction of the room where her father waited. "I bet not."

At that point, farm walls without insulation did their deed. Dr. Stone came flying out of the studio and practically ran up the short hall to the parlor where they were talking.

"You had it coming, Karen," he shouted at her. "You broke our hearts. We gave you everything. You could have had your pick of men. Your mother never got over that scene. She died with that on her mind."

"I see you haven't changed, Father." She looked sad and her face clouded over. "You still can't get past your prestigious community standing. My happiness means nothing to you. It just might get in the way of your making more money. That is all you care about. I thought maybe . . . Oh, never mind. I want you to leave now."

Without looking back, Dr. Stone hastily left the house, leaving the front door ajar. Karen firmly pushed it shut behind him.

They heard the engine noise as his car went flying up the lane, stones and dirt scattering behind it. Tires screeched when contact was made on the paved road above the farm. Looking out the front window, Mike could see the headlights heading back toward town.

Sheski took his seat again and the detectives waited for Karen to calm down. She walked into the kitchen, silently made coffee for all of them, and invited the policemen to sit around an oak pedestal table. She brought cups of dark, aromatic coffee for the three of them and placed them on individual placemats. Sheski stirred his coffee and stared at the Bucknell University bison on his mug.

Mike got out of his chair to look at the various pieces of artwork on the knotty pine walls. There were colorful watercolors of children and local points of interest, but what had his attention was a two-by-two oil painting hanging above a pine dry sink filled with cut glass.

A *P* could be seen in the lower left corner of the scene, with a child's face staring out from the loop. So detailed and realistic was the visage inside the capital letter, that viewing the tiny angelic face alone was worth the look.

Noticing his interest in the artwork, Karen said, "The watercolors are mine. I did them. That's an original Pratt you're looking at," she explained. "It was a birthday present to me from my parents." She then proceeded to tell the lieutenants the gruesome Pratt history, ending by explaining the value and rarity of his artwork. "There are only a few paintings around," she went on to say. "The historical society has them all catalogued if you're interested in learning more about them."

"I saw some of his work at the hospital, in the halls and in your father's office," Sheski said. "It's hard to believe that such a disturbed person could produce such fabulous art."

"Sometimes all that manic energy can produce artistic results. Remember Van Gogh," Karen said. "He was insane, too, but produced the most sought-after paintings of all time."

"Your grounds here at the farm are beautiful, too," Sheski said. He was a little surprised when Karen told him that John Deadly had prepared the layout for her landscaping.

"He doesn't look as if he would know anything about flowers, but he is brilliant with plant placement and landscaping. He designed the ponds here, also. When he found out that I had purchased this place, he volunteered his expertise. I couldn't pass it up. He's that good."

That man is full of surprises, thought Sheski.

Karen appeared relaxed, so Mike redirected the conversation to their investigation. "Can you tell us where Jess Walter is?" he asked.

Karen explained to the detectives that Jess had been at Bucknell University working all day. She also told them of her unsuccessful efforts to contact him. She no sooner finished her sentence when a vehicle was heard coming down the driveway toward the house.

"That had better not be Father again," Karen said. "If it is, go tell him I don't want to see him right now. No, wait. I'll tell him myself," she said determinedly, getting out of her chair.

Sheski went to the kitchen window, hoping it wasn't Dr. Stone. He looked out, turned back to Karen, and said, "It's a new black sport utility vehicle."

"Thank God," Karen said soberly. "That's Jess." She hastened to the door to greet him.

Jess Walter parked next to the lieutenants' car and came through a side door. He was about five-feet-eight-inches tall. A good-looking black man, who appeared to be in some distress.

Karen threw herself into his arms when he got inside the house. Jess lovingly held her, looking anxiously over her shoulder at the two men at the kitchen table. They, in turn, were looking back.

Eyes widened, Karen looked at Jess. "Where have you been?" she asked. "I've been trying to get a hold of you."

"And so have we," Sheski said.

"I've been working at my office. I haven't felt good for the past couple of hours so I took a short nap at my desk. I still don't feel well, Karen, I need to lie down," he said wearily. Murmuring an apology, he wandered down the hall to a bedroom.

"Can you please come back another time?" Karen awkwardly asked of the policemen. Looking anxious, she advanced to the door and opened it for them.

Mike and Sheski exchanged skeptical glances but agreed to return when Jess was feeling better. "We'll keep you posted with any news we may have, Karen. We'll be talking to you and Mr. Walter again . . . soon."

Karen nervously observed the staties get into their car and exit the driveway onto the upper road. Only after she was sure they were really gone did she hasten to the bedroom for an explanation.

Chapter Nine

Lana awoke early, feeling better and eager to enjoy her day off. In her robe and slippers, she stepped out onto the porch to retrieve her morning paper. The headline was not going to make Tommy happy, she thought. "DANVILLE SOCIALITE MURDERED," it said in big block letters. Underneath that provocative headline, in smaller type, was a zinger. "Town Fearful as Police Investigate." A large picture of a much younger Mrs. Rose Stone peered out from the center of the page with a caption noting her numerous charitable activities. Lana read the article twice, paying particular attention to their mention of her own role in the nightmare. She put it aside when she found herself getting a headache.

After working for a couple of hours on Stone Haven paperwork, Lana had the remainder of the weekend free to pursue her personal interests.

She fed Bunky, who was prancing around her heels,

and went upstairs to get ready for the day's activities. After showering and putting on makeup, she donned blue jeans, a scarlet Rutgers sweatshirt, socks, and black leather boots. Small gold earrings and a bracelet and watch finished off her outfit.

Lana observed herself in the mirror and was pleased with what she saw. Counting calories was an every-meal event in order to keep her trim figure, but it paid off. She still carried her high school weight and could get into her old cheerleading outfit.

She was looking forward to meeting her friends at the The Bridge Stop, their favorite diner, for their 11 A.M. soup and coffee klatch. She turned to hurry down the curved stairway and picked her gold cross off her jewelry box. Saying a silent prayer for the murderer's apprehension, she placed it about her neck.

Ever since Lana had returned to town, the group of old friends met on Saturday mornings at the same window table of the diner. Included in the group besides Lana were Connie Thomas, Barbara Clark, and Cindy Fox. Connie's friendship with Lana was the longest and dearest. Their relationship went back to the third grade at the now-razed brick school in Riverside where they clapped erasers together on the iron fire escape and played jump rope at recess.

Connie was married for thirty-plus years to her high school sweetheart and had two children. A petite blond, the once-skinny classmate of Lana's now was plump. She didn't care. Her job as a clerk at the Montour County courthouse and her family kept her too busy to worry about the extra pounds. Besides, her husband loved her just the way she was. Connie was fun to be with and could be counted on to keep a secret. Their friendship had endured Lana's departure to college and years of working in other cities. When Lana returned to town, they picked up as if they had never been separated.

Barbara Clark, a first grade schoolteacher, was also with Lana and Connie in the class of '65 at Danville High School. The three of them had been cheerleaders together, and shared many fond memories of their school years. Unlike Connie, Barbara was quiet and introspective, though somewhat nosy. The brown-eyed brunet still kept her slim figure, much to the happiness of her accountant husband, John. This was Barbara's second marriage, neither of which had produced children. That was by choice. She enjoyed teaching everyone else's offspring, but wanted peace and quiet when she came home.

Cindy Fox was the last of the foursome. Cindy was a year younger than the other friends, something which she happily held over their heads like a hammer. When birthdays rolled around she reminded them that she was the youngest of the group. They all had a good laugh about it and would kid her that she looked older than they, so it didn't really matter. Cindy was tall, willowy, and a natural redhead. A business major, she had married her college sweetheart. Together they had opened a restaurant/motel on the edge of town, which flourished until she caught her husband of five years in bed in room 113 with their accountant. The shock of the confrontation nearly killed her. She wouldn't come out of her house for two weeks, barely eating a thing. If it weren't for the good friends gathered with her today, she would probably still be there. They'd dragged her out of bed, bathed, dressed, fed her, and cried with her. With their help, Cindy had the strength to recover and face the future. She convinced her husband to quietly sign over the business and divorce papers, and she hadn't looked back. Presently, she had been dating an old school friend who was now a partner in a law firm in Williamsport. The last she heard of her ex, he had moved to Harrisburg and opened a small gift shop.

Lana thought about her friends and hurried to finish getting ready. Bunky followed her around the bedroom while his owner dressed, hoping something, anything, would fall to the floor so he could grab it and run. That was his favorite game. Napkins, teabags, socks—anything that made its way to his level was fair game. He had it in his tiny jaws before the owner even knew it had fallen. He would walk slowly up to the person, show them his treasure, and then run all over the house hoping to be chased. It was impossible to catch him. He would sprint with the item, under the furniture, dodging his pursuer, and generally having a great time. If the chaser wore out and stopped playing, he would come back to within a foot or two of them and dare to be chased again. Many times, the stolen item would end up hidden from view under the couch or a chair. He was disappointed today because nothing was dropped.

This morning, Lana was feeling a little better despite not getting a full night's rest. Throughout her slumber, she kept awakening at intervals when nocturnal house noises invaded her sleep, causing her to look fearfully about the bedroom for God knows what. At 3 A.M., she actually got out of bed and made a sweep of the house, starting in the cellar, due to a creaking noise she could not identify. From the dining room window, she had peered out at the carriage house and saw movement in the shadows. *Get hold of yourself,* she'd thought. *It's only your imagination.* Just to make sure, she turned all the lights out and watched again for a few minutes. Nothing. Light from the gas station across the street lit up the fronts of the white barn and shed at the edge of her property. All looked okay. Visions of Rose's murdered body and the bloodied kitchen further impeded her ability to return to sleep. Finally, in desperation, she turned on the small noise machine on her nightstand, which filtered out any further sounds, and fell into a deep sleep to the sound of gently-crashing ocean waves. A sleep which was uninterrupted until the alarm went off at 6 A.M. the next morning.

Lana had about an hour before her friends were expecting her. She decided to walk across the river bridge to town, something she enjoyed, and do some banking and mail letters.

Crossing the Susquehanna on the worn-out steel bridge, Lana was glad that the sun was shining and the air was crisp and clear. A gentle wind was blowing small whitecaps, which lapped against the stone bridge supports as she walked briskly. Her mind was focused intently on what she would tell her friends about Rose's death. They would know about it by now and would expect a first-person account from her. How much could she tell them? How much should she tell them? These questions nagged at her. She hated the thought of having to recount the gory details. She was so deep in thought that she didn't hear a vehicle stop and discharge someone who began walking behind her on the concrete walkway. When she stopped to look over the railing at the water below, Lana noticed that, about one span behind her, someone else was looking at the river, also. It appeared to be a small man dressed in dark clothing. Although she couldn't see his face, which was turned away from her, she felt as though the person was someone familiar.

Taking her gloved hands from her coat pockets, she resumed her walk. She was cognizant that the man did the same. *I must be getting paranoid,* she thought. *If I keep this up, I'll need a tranquilizer. That experience yesterday has me scared to death. A lot of people walk this bridge,* she reasoned. Especially since a new bridge was under construction nearby. Lana turned to view the unfinished concrete span being built about 300 feet downstream. Regardless of her rationalizing the circumstances, she picked up her pace and was alarmed to note that the person behind her did, too.

She continued across the bridge, sprinting the rest of the way to the post office in the center of town. She was out of breath and her hair windblown to an unrecognizable mess. Hurrying through the entrance, she looked back over her shoulder as if expecting someone to come through the doorway after her.

The lobby was full as usual on a Saturday morning. Alice Fry, owner of a dry cleaning shop, was waiting in line and yelled a greeting to her as she deposited some letters in the "Danville Only" slot. Lana managed a tight smile and waved in return. She quickly exited through glass doors and down the marble steps to the sidewalk.

The bank was Lana's last stop before crossing the bridge back to Riverside to get her car. She looked quickly about to see if she was being followed. Seeing no one, she briskly walked the incline up to the bridge, holding on to the cold handrail. She gazed at the length of walkway ahead of her to the other side of the river and, seeing it empty, started her journey across the murky water.

Walking swiftly, Lana's attention was riveted on her destination at the end of the bridge. Only seven spans, she told herself, and I'll be off this thing. Offering a prayer, her heart pounding, she put three spans behind her. About the middle of the fourth one, Lana peered over her shoulder and was horrified to again see a dark-clothed figure about fifty feet behind her. Occasionally glancing backward, her stride a near-run, she almost knocked an approaching grade school bike rider off his blue two wheeler. The little boy scowled at an apologetic Lana, adjusted his wobbly pace and continued on. So did the dark figure. By the time she made it to the end of the bridge, she was out of breath, gasping and leaning over the decline railing. She looked back from where she had come and saw that the bridge was empty. *Could I have imagined that?* she asked herself. Heart pounding, Lana quickly crossed the railroad tracks and entered the barn to get her car. Driving back across the bridge, she strained to see if the dark-clothed figure was still there. She was relieved to see no one.

The restaurant owner smiled and waved to Lana as she abruptly made her way to her three friends, who were seated at their favorite window table. Lana waved in return. "You look like you've seen a ghost," Connie said, getting up to hug her closest friend. "Are you all right? And why didn't you call us after the ordeal you've been through? The murder and all. We'd have come over to stay with you."

"I'm okay," Lana answered uncertainly, holding onto Connie for dear life. "I guess I'm a little spooked after yesterday's events."

She pulled herself away and removed her green car coat. She sat down with the others and tried to regain her composure. The foursome ordered their coffee and homemade soups. When the waitress left, the three friends looked expectantly at the exhausted Lana for her version of the murder. The gruesome tale of finding Rose's body was recounted, uninterrupted, concluding with her suspicions that she was being watched and followed. Lana leaned back in her chair, looked anxiously into her friend's faces, and waited for some feedback. She needed to hear from them.

"Oh Lana, that must have been horrible for you," Connie blurted out. "We should be mad at you for not calling us!"

"I don't know why I didn't," she said softly. "I should have. Now that we're all together, I feel better. I'm sure there's nothing to worry about." She gave a small laugh, which did nothing to ease their minds. Questions were asked and answered between bites of muffins and sips of soup. Lana answered what she could and speculation began on who could have been the murderer.

"Well, we know it wasn't you who killed Rose," Cindy said. "You've broken a few hearts, but that's about all the harm you could do to someone. Mrs. Stone, on the other hand, now that's another story. She may have been a tireless worker for improving the town, but she made a lot of enemies along the way. Her with her superior, snobby attitude toward the locals, waving her expensive jewelry in everyone's faces." Cindy lowered her voice conspiratorially. "Especially that five-carat ring."

"Nine," corrected Lana. "Nine-carat. Whoever took that really got a prize. She told me more than once that it was worth more than most people would earn in a lifetime."

Barbara countered, "Well, maybe it was, but most people in this town didn't like her. She was always trying to strong arm someone into accepting her restoration ideas. And, because of her wealth, she was able to get her way most of the time. I know that some of the Mill Street property owners were not enamored with her plans to restore all of the storefronts to their original facades. It would have cost them plenty and lost revenue, too, if Rose would have lived to make the Restoration Committee meeting Friday night. I hear that's when she was going to present the final Mill Street plan, armed with the bids and projected expenses. If she would have been there she would have muscled it through."

The others nodded their heads in agreement.

"The committee members wouldn't have wanted to go against her," Barbara continued. "As it happened, they didn't know about her murder and gladly went ahead with their meeting without her. Bobby Snyder was in here earlier and I heard him telling some of his buddies that, without Rose there to protest, the committee voted down the storefront idea. 'It's as dead as Rose,' he told them."

Lana grimaced at such a callous remark.

Connie added, "Talk about coldhearted. Maybe he didn't get along with her, but he could have been a little more compassionate. He complained that her idea would have wiped him out since he owns half of the buildings on the west side of the street. He was sure Rose couldn't have gotten enough grant money to assist the owners in complying with what would have been mandated."

The friends all knew Bobby. He had been a trouble-maker when he was a small boy. Wild and wily, he was usually behind any mischief that was going on in school or at the local playground. When a BB shot out a street light, the town police knew to go to his house if they wanted the culprit. Of course, that was a long time ago, when there were fewer kids in town and the police knew them all by name.

As a teenager, Bobby would occasionally skip school and go fishing in the creek or along the river. Twice he was caught stealing from school lockers, and most people were surprised when he managed to grad-uate. Bobby's father was one of the high school custodians and his mother worked in the cafeteria. His parents were good people who did what they could to handle their incorrigible son.

"I remember that after graduation, he went off to Vietnam and then stayed in the army for a while," Cindy said. "While there, he served with Lesley Stone and some of the other locals. I don't know what went on over there, but when they all eventually returned, it was clear that something had turned them against each other. It was probably Bobby's fault," she said judgmentally.

"Bobby went on to make something of himself and I give him credit for that," Lana argued, defending her old classmate. "He worked hard and saved to buy the buildings that he owns. He's made a regular business out of room and storefront rentals. I can understand his being upset about Rose's plans. He didn't have the kind of money it would have taken to restore them."

"Leave it to you to defend someone like Bobby Snyder," Cindy said. "I remember how angry you used to get at him when we were kids and he tried to look up our dresses at recess."

The four friends started to laugh, looking back and forth at each other, until tears were rolling down their faces. Slowly they got control of themselves, and ate and talked while other patrons came and went.

"Bobby may not be a slumlord," Barbara said, "But he's close to it. He doesn't do much to fix up what he has. Even though he served on the Restoration Committee with Rose, he really hated her trying to force him to improve those properties. He kinda resented her wealth, too, but he was right, you know. If Rose wanted it done, she could afford to pay for all of it herself, as rich as she was."

"Well, he didn't look guilty of anything but getting his own way when I saw him earlier," said Connie. "You guys are too hard on him. He's become a respectable adult and deserves the benefit of the doubt. Hey, I remember when you had a crush on him in third grade and we tried to make the two of you kiss," she said laughingly to Cindy. "You used to run from us, but I know you really wanted to do it."

With that, the friends convulsed again with laughter while Cindy good-naturedly screwed her face up and stuck her tongue out at them.

When the laughter died down, Lana said, "I know that Rose was trying to help Bobby with the cost. She wrote proposals and made contacts to bring that about. After seeing the bid sheets, though, it still would have cost property owners a lot if she had had her way. I guess Bobby has some reason to be pleased it fell through."

It was at that point that Lana realized her companions weren't really paying attention to her anymore. Instead, they were staring over her shoulder at someone who was standing behind her, listening to their conversation. With a start, Lana jerked her head around to see who it was.

"I'm sorry to have startled you," a smiling Lieutenant Sheski stated. "You look really frightened." He seemed concerned, yet happy to see her.

"I'm still a little jumpy from yesterday," Lana said

carefully. She hoped that she didn't have food on her face and that her hair looked okay. She absently smoothed hair out of her eyes and smiled at him, avoiding eye contact with her friends. She could feel three pairs of questioning orbs staring at her and the detective.

"What are you doing here?" she asked.

"Mike and I were in town working and thought we'd come in for lunch. He had to leave a little early so I stayed to enjoy the coffee. Then I saw you."

Lana's companions were all looking at her with expectant faces, as though an introduction should be the next step. "Oh, excuse me," Lana said, a little embarrassed. "Let me introduce you to my friends, Tommy." At the mention of "Tommy," the three high school chums shared knowing glances back and forth. Introductions were made all around and Lana could see that they were impressed with him.

It was plain that the lieutenant was a little uncomfortable with all the attention, shifting back and forth from one foot to another and glancing around. Lana excused herself from her table and rescued him by asking if they could have a word in private.

"Glad to," he said. "Excuse us, please," he said to the others with a smile.

While her friends stared, both of them stepped to the back of the restaurant, out of earshot of the patrons.

"I don't know if it's my imagination or not," began Lana, "But I get the feeling that I'm being watched and followed." She slowly recounted her sleep-deprived night and the events on the bridge that morning.

Sheski listened intently, his handsome face sober. "I can assign someone to keep a watch on you for a while," he said when she was finished. "At least until we find out if there's anything to this. Just to be on the safe side."

"I don't want a bodyguard staying with me or following me around," she said, a bit annoyed. "Now that I've told you, I feel foolish. I'm sure that it's nothing, just my imagination."

Lieutenant Sheski wasn't so sure. He tried to protest, but Lana was firm.

"At least let me stop by later tonight to make sure you're all right," he asked.

Lana thought a minute and said that would be okay. She even welcomed it. The lieutenant was a really nice guy. She admired his intelligence and the respectful manner he showed to others. Those qualities were important to her. Although looks weren't a prerequisite to getting a date with her, it didn't hurt that he was handsome. She had noticed that he wasn't wearing a wedding ring and remembered someone remarking at the murder scene that he was single.

"Would you like to come for dinner?" she asked.

He flushed a little and said, "I'd like that. What time?"

"How about seven?"

"That would be great," he said. "Believe it or not, I can make my own meals, but cooking for one gets tiresome sometimes and I don't like eating alone."

That gave Lana some insight into his availability.

She motioned for him to look out the back door window and across the river to the large white home near the bridge.

"That's mine," she said. "Remember to ring the front doorbell so I can hear you in case I'm in the back of the house," she advised.

They rejoined her friends and Sheski gave his apologies for having to go. Lana accompanied him to the cashier and watched as he paid his bill and then went to his car. There were three sets of raised eyebrows and grins when she got back to their table.

"Tommmmmy, is it?" teased Barbara. "Why didn't you tell us about him? He's gorgeous." The three women murmured their approval.

"There's really nothing to tell," Lana said with a half-smile. "He's one of the investigators assigned to the murder, that's all. He's a lieutenant in the state police department." She reached for her coffee and tried to change the topic by remarking on how good the regular diner coffee was.

"Yeah, right, nothing to tell," said Connie. "You've been keeping secrets from me." The others rolled their eyes in disbelief and started to laugh.

"What's Evan going to think?" Barbara interjected. The others stopped and looked at her, not sure where she was going with this remark.

"Why should it matter?" Connie interjected defensively. "She's not seeing him anymore," her best friend said, turning to face her. "Are you?"

"Not since May," Lana replied quietly, looking

about her to make sure other customers weren't listening. "It just wasn't working out. He's really nice, but I don't love him. I just didn't want to lead him on, that's all."

Barbara was staring at something in the opposite corner. "Well, I hear he's still carrying a torch for you, my friend," she said mockingly.

"He still calls once in awhile to talk," Lana offered. "But we're not seeing each other anymore."

"Well brace yourself, honey," Barbara said stiffly, " 'cuz attorney Evan Haynes is coming this way."

The four friends turned to where Barbara had been staring and saw the fiftyish, medium height, dark-haired lawyer advancing toward them. He was wearing a suit with a topcoat and kept his eyes on Lana, pausing a couple of times to say hello to others dining nearby. His black monogrammed attache case swung back and forth as he walked ever closer.

"Hello, Lana," he said, looking her full in the eyes. "Hi guys," he said to the others.

They all murmured a hello back. Lana asked him how he was and invited him to sit with them.

"I can't stay, I'm late for a meeting now, maybe another time," Evan replied. "Did I see you talking to Lieutenant Sheski a few minutes ago?" he asked.

Lana's face reddened a little and she nodded her head. "Do you know him?" she asked, averting her eyes to look at the muffin she was eating.

"We've met professionally a couple of times. He's a good guy. Smart, too. I was part of the investigating team when his wife was killed." Pausing, he added, "Are you two seeing each other or something?"

Without answering him directly, Lana answered, "He's the investigator assigned to the Rose Stone murder." She wanted to ask him about Tommy's wife but decided against it.

"Oh yeah, I heard about that. Are you all right? That must have been terrible for you."

"It was. But I'm okay now."

"I'd gladly come over and help in any way I can," he offered, waiting for her response.

"You know I'd call if I needed to," Lana said.

Evan looked disappointed. "Well, I've gotta go," he said, looking at his watch. "Remember, if you need anything, some advice, or just to talk, just give me a call, okay?" he said to Lana, hopefully. Evan looked in her eyes for just a moment, turned to the others, and said, "I'll see ya." He then walked briskly through the same door that Sheski through which exited earlier.

Lana looked at her friends, who were looking back at her.

"He's still got it for you," Barbara said in a singsongy tone. "I can tell."

"I hope not," Lana countered. "He's really a nice guy and deserves someone who feels the same way about him."

"How about this Tommy guy," Barbara added. "What's he to you?"

"Nothing. We just met," she said, defending herself

again. "Besides," she joked, "My personal life is none of your business anyway. Not that he's in my personal life . . . Not that I have a personal life . . . Not that I'm interested in him or anything." The hole Lana was digging got deeper and deeper.

Chapter Ten

Gordon Ashman, great-grandson of Andrew Ashman, founder of the now-defunct Danville Iron Mill, had the same good business sense as the Ashman males before him. Educated at Harvard, the wealthy fifty-two-year-old collector of Civil War memorabilia had even managed to turn his hobby into a successful venture.

The gray granite Ashman mansion at the edge of Danville was stately and imposing in both size and style. It was unmistakable to visitors, though, that the house was a lived-in home. The furnishings, tasteful collectibles, were comfortable and inviting to those who came through the double walnut front doors. Civil War catalogs and history books were strewn about the den. The large home came complete with a ballroom that was built during the heyday of the iron industry by the company founder. In a gesture similar to those of great men before him, he erected the home as a tribute to his wife Ella, the love of his life. A large, ornate iron fence, decorated with peacocks, surrounded the property. The design was a one of a kind his foundry produced just for her, despite requests from other wealthy families.

"You can't have it," he would say. "That pattern is for my Ella." Then he would smile lovingly at her, and she at him.

In addition to inheriting the Ashman property, Gordon had inherited his great-grandfather's innate intelligence, good character, and wisdom. He was well-respected throughout his community, and for good reason. Gordon was what was once referred to as a gentleman. He was a kind, faithful husband to his wife Gladys, and a good father to their two sons and daughter.

Gordon was in the study reading a Civil War journal, trying to take his mind off the recent murder. Gladys quietly entered the room.

"We must be going, darling," she said gently to her husband. "I telephoned Lesley to let him know that we would soon be stopping by to spend some time with him. How awful for him and Karen. They must be so upset."

She touched his shoulder affectionately before leaving the room to get her coat.

Gladys, of average height and build with a pretty face framed by soft brown hair, moved about with the grace of a dancer. An avid golfer, she had spent some time at the club with Rose. They had also served on the boards of several local charities together. Gladys lacked Rose's pushiness and pomposity but they shared a fondness for the town. She was friendly to Dr. Stone's wife as she was to most people, but, because of their personality differences, didn't count Rose among her closest friends.

Gordon joined his wife in the foyer and helped her on with her coat. Standing under the brass chandelier centered near the doorway, he pulled her close and silently thanked God for her. He could feel her gentle warmth beneath the leather. He never tired of touching her.

Despite his wealth, Gordon knew his real treasure was his loved ones. He also knew that Lesley Stone did not feel the same about his family. He had heard the rumors about town, had seen the knowing looks amongst club members at their tables when Lesley and Kylie Burns were having lunch together. He was disgusted at the thought of Lesley carrying on with his own partner's wife. And Kylie was even one of Rose's friends. Twice he had accidentally walked in on them at Lesley's office, their clothes askew and her make-up smudged. Embarrassed, he had made hasty exits, promising to call Lesley later.

His own friend's wife. How could he do that? Gordon wondered. *And what about Rose?* He shuddered to think what Rose would have done had she known. Well, he didn't have to worry about that now. She would never know. At the thought of his friend's predicament, Gordon gave Gladys an extra strong hug.

She smiled up at him, unaware of the source of her husband's tight embrace.

"We should be going now. Lesley and Karen will need to have friends with them at this time," she said, not really wanting to interrupt the moment.

Chapter Eleven

Lesley Stone had been receiving friends and neighbors at his home in the Sweetriver development all Saturday evening. They called or arrived to express their condolences and offer assistance. Some came hoping to get a glimpse of the now-sanitized crime scene. A few were disappointed to find that all traces of the murder had been cleansed from the kitchen.

A special cleaning crew had been dispatched by the Stones' house-cleaning service as soon as the police released the area back to the psychiatrist. Rose's lifeless body was now resting at the funeral home, awaiting private services and then burial.

Lesley gave a brief thought to how he would dispose of her belongings. *I could probably sell them somewhere and make out pretty good,* he thought. *Rose always bought the best.* He brushed it off, figuring he'd take care of that later, when he had some privacy.

Rose would have hated a public viewing, he thought. She never went anywhere unless she was meticulously groomed and dressed. With that damned diamond ever-present on her right hand. Where was that diamond? He wanted it back.

There was already a small gathering at the Stone residence when, at 6:15 P.M., on his way to Lana's, Lieutenant Sheski waved his badge at the Sweetriver guard shack. He knew that he could get to his date with Lana by 7 P.M., if he left here by 6:50.

Sheski drove his late model beige Cougar up to the front of the Stones' home and parked. He straightened his tie, cleared his throat, and walked toward the house. He could feel the crisp fall chill in the air and looked up at the clear, star-filled sky.

Approaching the sidewalk, he observed the beautiful tile and glass artwork beneath his feet. Looking down in awe, he understood what had entranced Lana the day of Rose's murder. The entire walkway was luminescent, lit up from some invisible light source beneath it. It enabled the visitors not only to see their way to the house but also to have something to admire. The effect was breathtaking.

Upon reaching the front door, Sheski took one last look back the way he came, rang the doorbell, and waited for an answer.

For the lieutenant, this was purely a social call, but if he observed anything that could be used in an official capacity, all the better.

It was not uncommon for detectives to make a social

call on a murder victim's family. After all, they would be working closely with them to bring the murderer to justice. Expressing condolences at a gathering such as this could aid in getting to know each other.

The door was opened with a "Good Evening" from a uniformed butler, who took the lieutenant's dark overcoat and motioned to the living room, where Dr. Stone was busy with friends.

Sheski walked slowly through the large rooms, past guests milling quietly about with porcelain cups and hors d'oeuvre plates in hand. He noticed that some were making small talk, heads close together, while others stood silently, unsure of what to say.

Sheski managed to overhear some conversations praising Dr. Stone for his commitment to his clients. They spoke of how brilliantly he managed the patients' dosage of psychiatric medications and therapy sessions. His dedication to their recovery and well-being was made a top priority.

Nearby, the lieutenant saw Jerry Smithson handing his business card to an uptight young couple. Jerry explained his firm's operation to the young man, patting him on the back for emphasis. The couple looked uncomfortable. Jerry appeared not to notice.

Sheski approached the recently-widowed psychiatrist, and, with an outstretched hand, murmured, "Please accept my heartfelt condolences, Dr. Stone."

The doctor looked a little surprised to see him, but shook the offered hand warmly after assurances it was not a professional call, but strictly social.

"Thank you for coming, Lieutenant. It means a lot to me to know that you are on the case. Please, make yourself at home." He displayed the sad countenance of grieving. "You must come visit me again after all of this is over. I could show you around and we could talk about more pleasant topics then."

Sheski wordlessly nodded his head.

The doctor looked about self-consciously to see if others recognized the policeman. When apparently none did, the relieved host introduced Sheski to Dr. and Mrs. Richard Burns, who were standing near a lighted display case, and then went to greet some new arrivals.

Sheski observed uniformed help walking about offering refreshments to the many callers in the home. People from all walks of life were present. Most looked well-heeled, but some of Rose's acquaintances from her various charitable groups were also there.

Some guests talked in low tones amongst themselves regarding Rose's many contributions to her community, praising the deceased as if she were a saint. Others couldn't keep their eyes off the art deco treasures. Jade, onyx, and bronze pieces were tastefully arranged about the house. Carved ivory nudes from Wenzel in Berlin, Deckel in Munich, and Kempf in Taunis were displayed in a lit, black lacquered display cabinet. An enviable collection.

An original Dupas painting of an elaborately dressed woman clutching her jewelry box was featured in the formal dining room. While admiring it, Sheski felt a light touch on his back. He turned to see a familiar face smiling back.

"How have you been?" Evan Hayes asked.

"Well," replied Sheski.

"Good," Evan replied sincerely. "Here as a friend, or is this a fact-finding mission?"

"Looking for answers. I never knew these people before Rose Stone's murder. How about you?"

"Strictly social. Rose and I co-chaired a charity together. She was one of a kind."

"So I've heard," Sheski replied sarcastically.

"Oh yeah, I hear Lana Stahl discovered the body," Evan remarked casually, watching Sheski's expression.

Sheski sensed that Evan knew something. "Yes, she did. It was quite a shock for her. You know Lana?" he asked inquisitively.

"We use to go out together." He looked around before saying, "That was awhile ago. How about you? You seeing anyone?"

Sheski was unsure how to answer that but chose a truthful, though evasive reply. "Not really."

Before he could go on, Jerry Smithson walked by and, spying Evan, queried, "Where are you on the Courter divorce? I've been waiting for your reply on our proposal."

Sheski was glad for the interruption. He wasn't sure where Evan's questioning might head and didn't really want to discuss Lana with him.

Jerry had Evan on the defensive and Sheski said, "Later," to his old acquaintance and moved out into the foyer. Evan sighed and huddled with Smithson in a corner.

Despite the appeal of the many treasures, most people eventually gravitated to a four-by-six oil on canvas in the foyer. It was a painting of three small, blond girls with sad little smiles. They were dressed in turn-of-the-century finery and playing with porcelain-bodied dolls.

Sheski, too, was drawn to it. The angelic innocence of the young children, their fingernails painted daintily in bright colors, and the detail of the artwork were compelling. As his eyes crossed the picture he noticed, in the left corner, the unmistakable Pratt signature. A large *P* with a whimsical child's face in the loop.

"Do you like it?" a man's voice inquired from behind. Lieutenant Sheski turned and was surprised to see John Deadly eyeing him. The security man was absently manipulating some of the flowers in arrangements that had been sent to the home earlier in the day.

"Why, yes, I do," he replied evenly. "However, knowing the Pratt history, it seems a bit morbid."

Sheski saw Deadly's face cloud at his response.

"Do you know how rare a Pratt is?" Deadly said pompously. "Few are found outside the hospital walls. I could count on one hand the households that boast an original. None are in museums despite their attempts to get their hands on one. Pratts are passed from generation to generation in this town. Children fight over who will inherit them. Oliver Pratt took almost a year to paint each one, no matter the size. They are meticulous in design and detail." He paused. "Experts believe that the children he painted were his victims."

He awaited the effect of this last statement on the lieutenant. Sheski's flat expression did not change.

"His scenes of early life on the Susquehanna river show extraordinary detail," Deadly went on. "The details document the minutiae of his time. Look how beautifully he captures the landscaping along the waterway." His eyes glistened, transfixed on the canvas. He beamed with pride, which Sheski believed was due to his knowledge of art.

"Pratt must have had some mobility during his hospitalization in order to accomplish all that," Sheski said.

Studying the smaller man, the detective observed that this was the first time he had seen him out of uniform. And in a suit, no less, and without that tam. He looked smaller than his already diminutive size but no less intimidating. He had an air of calm authority which he wore brazenly. *This is a man who is used to telling people what to do and knowing how to get them to do it,* Sheski observed. *It probably has something to do with his military background.*

"What did this guy look like?" asked Sheski quizzically. "Did he ever paint his own picture?"

"Pratt wrote in his journal that he only painted one self-portrait. He considered himself a small, unattractive man and didn't like mirrors or his picture taken."

Sheski looked sharply at Deadly, realizing that the man must had read the dilapidated Pratt journal.

Deadly's voice then took on an unmistakable edge. "Not to change the subject, but is this a social call, or professional?"

The quick change of tone and subject surprised Sheski, who quickly, too quickly, replied, "Strictly social. This was a cold-blooded murder of a woman and I just wanted to pay my respects to the family."

Sheski wondered to himself why he felt as if he had to answer Deadly. He had been caught off guard. That didn't happen too often, and he didn't like it when it did.

He glanced at his watch, met Deadly's stern gaze, and said, "I must be going. It's been interesting. Oh, I'll be coming around to see you soon." He paused. "Professionally. I have some questions to ask you . . . on the record."

"I'll be ready," Deadly said, bristling.

A casual observer couldn't have missed the animosity between the two.

Sheski despised Deadly's air of superiority and threatening looks, his strut, and his cold, knowing stare.

Deadly viewed Sheski as an enemy. Someone who was bullying his way into his turf. After all, he was the head of security at Stone Haven. *I probably make more money than that gumshoe could dream of,* Deadly thought cockily. *And I'm worth it.*

Sheski was walking toward the library to retrieve his coat when he caught sight of Dr. Stone and Kylie Burns huddled behind one of the etched blue-glass library doors. Whispering intently, they did not see him coming. The taller psychiatrist was affectionately looking down at the smaller, attractive woman. His right arm was around her tiny waist, though he quickly drew it away when he sensed someone was nearby.

"Excuse me," Sheski said noncommittally to both

Lesley and Kylie. "I was just leaving. Again, please accept my condolences, Dr. Stone. I'll be in touch."

The doctor self-consciously replied, "Thank you, I'll look forward to hearing from you."

Kylie stepped back and gave neither man eye contact.

The Ashmans arrived shortly before 7 P.M. as Sheski was leaving. They came through the door, were introduced to him, and asked if there was anything they could do to assist with the investigation.

"If so, please call anytime," Gordon instructed him.

Sheski assured the couple that if he needed them, they would be contacted. They then turned their attention to their bereaved friend.

Gordon and Gladys hugged their friend, murmuring words of sorrow and offering to help in any way. Lesley thanked the couple, turned to scrutinize Sheski's departure, and invited them into his living room.

"We're so sorry," Gladys murmured. "It's such a tragedy. How is Karen? Is she here yet?"

"She won't be coming. This has been overwhelming for her and she is at her home trying to cope," he replied tonelessly.

Neither of the Ashmans believed him. They knew of the Stones' estrangement from their daughter and the circumstances surrounding it.

Gordon had tried unsuccessfully to talk sense into Lesley and Rose about their daughter's engagement right after it happened. Rose wouldn't even discuss it. She indicated her confidence that Karen would come to her senses, knowing she would get nothing further from them unless she did. Rose even went so far as to say that she would soon be consulting a lawyer to make some changes in her will.

Lesley was present when Rose told this to them. He had wondered how he could be surrounded by women who wanted to give their money away—first his mother and now his wife.

When Karen mended her ways, Rose went on, the will would be changed back and her daughter would inherit her mother's estate. The Ashmans knew there would be no further discussion about the issue and did not mention it again. They believed that the Stones could be a headstrong family.

Gordon and Gladys couldn't imagine being estranged from one's own child, but they knew that the topic was closed. Both of them thought it tragic that Rose went to her death without repairing the relationship. Incomprehensible.

Chapter Twelve

Sheski arrived at Lana's home and rang the doorbell at the front door, as she had instructed him earlier. He looked at the circular porch of the Victorian building that went around the right side of the house and thought it charming.

From inside, the shrill bark of a small dog could be heard. He waited and shortly the front door opened.

"Hi, Tommy," Lana said.

Sheski couldn't believe how good she looked. She was wearing makeup and had pulled her hair back from her attractive face, showing off big green eyes. Her trim figure was accentuated in a plain long black form-fitting collarless dress, open at the neck. He sputtered a hello and handed her a bunch of flowers that he had purchased earlier.

Lana invited him in, thanked him for the gift, and took his coat into her small library, where she laid it over a rocking chair. Bunky continued barking in the background until his owner took her guest in to meet him. He was confined to the back part of the house due to his habit of nibbling at her books and the fringe on the oriental carpets. The six-pound dog was dancing back and forth with glee at meeting a new friend.

He's anything but a watchdog, Sheski thought. *The only defense he could offer would be to warn of an intruder.* Sheski bent down to pet the dog, who showed obvious signs of enjoying the attention. He genuinely liked dogs and it showed. Lana was relieved to see that. She often made judgments about people based on whether they liked pets or not.

"All right, you've gotten your share of the attention," Lana said affectionately to her pet while picking the wriggling canine up. "Time for you to slow down." She placed him in the laundry room so she could check on their dinner.

"How was the rest of your day?" Sheski asked. He looked genuinely concerned.

"Not so good. My phone wouldn't stop ringing with calls from reporters who wanted to talk to me. I let the answering machine pick them up." She looked wistful. "I don't want to be interviewed. That was a horrible thing that happened, and I don't want to have to keep reliving it."

"I should have warned you about that. Reporters can be relentless. Don't return their calls until you're ready. If you want, I'll keep you company for moral support if and when you decide you want to talk to them."

"Thanks for the offer. I may take you up on it. Now, if you want to, take a look around the house while I get back to the kitchen."

Sheski wandered around the downstairs while his date puttered in the kitchen. Off to the right of the front hallway entrance, there was a large living room with a tiled fireplace. Victorian grass wallpaper with a ceiling border gave the room warmth.

Crossing the maroon rug, he entered the television room with the back stairway and went on through into the dining room. Wandering about the back of the house, he found Bunky in the laundry room contentedly curled up on a blanket-covered stool. The dog lifted his head sleepily and then rested it on his extended front paws. Sheski then checked out the kitchen again, where Lana was, oven mitts on, transferring food items to serving dishes. He watched her quietly, admiring her attractive face and figure for a half-minute and then retraced his steps to the front door.

Sheski walked into the library, stopping to inspect book titles on the white floor-to-ceiling shelving. History books lay next to poetry, mystery, and gardening. *Eclectic reading tastes,* he thought. He then went back into the kitchen, where he saw that Lana was almost ready to serve the meal.

Sheski noticed that she had decorated the kitchen table with the flowers he had given her. The blooms had been separated and placed in a crystal vase and the table was set with white linens and china.

He remarked on how nice everything looked, and

Lana gave him another big smile and a thank-you. "The china was my grandmother's," she said.

The meal tasted as good as it looked. Prime rib, baked potatoes with sour cream, and green beans with almonds were topped off with Lana's specialty . . . homemade chocolate cake.

They ate, making small talk and asking personal questions designed to fill in the gaps of information they lacked about each other. Lana learned that her date had a grown son, Thomas Jr.

Sheski told her about his wife Lois's death ten years ago.

This must be what Evan was referring to, Lana thought.

He explained that Lois had had a successful real estate business and they had just celebrated their twentieth anniversary. He paused often, eyes clouded over, telling how he had not taken his weapon when they had gone out that night to a movie.

"After the film was over, we got up to leave, when, a few rows in front of us, some boys began fighting over a girl. Most of the people had already left, but those who remained turned to see what was going on. It all happened so fast. The argument escalated swiftly and before we could react, shots were fired by one of the young boys. Lois was struck in the temple and died in my arms."

Sheski paused and Lana touched his hand in an effort to ease his pain. After a minute he continued.

"One of the teens, Louis, was convicted of murder and sent to a facility for juveniles, where he stayed until his eighteenth birthday. He was a troublemaker while locked up, and was transferred to a state penitentiary, where he remains today. The other teen made a deal, testified against Louis, and was released from the same lockup after serving only eighteen months."

"For many years I tortured myself with 'what if' questions. What if I had pulled her down to the floor when the fight started? What if we had chosen a differ-ent movie, a different day to go, a different theater? What if I had taken my gun?" Sheski looked miserable. "Maybe I could have broken it up before it got out of hand."

Lana's psychiatric nurse training took over and she listened silently as he finished.

Again, she touched his hand gently and asked thoughtfully about their son.

Sheski looked up at her, and said with a grin, "Our son Thomas went on to Penn State like his dad. He graduated with a degree in computer-something-or-the-other and now operates his own business in Laguna Beach, California. I'm proud of him. He's a nice young man, much like his mother. He's enjoying life in the sun out on the coast. We talk weekly and visit each other twice a year. I fly out there in April, and he flies east in October. That way we both get the best weather California and Pennsylvania have to offer. I enjoy the warm California climate and he gets to see the fall foliage. I miss him, but it works."

Lana, in turn, told him about her nursing career and the brief engagement she had while in college. Her fiancé, a med student, decided about two months before they were to be wed that he had made a mistake by not getting back together with his former girlfriend. Their engagement was broken, he married his ex and, broken-hearted, Lana finished college. After that, despite dating and romances, she had never committed herself again to another.

More talk ensued between them, interspersed with quiet tunes. For a first date, the few silences that occurred were not uncomfortable. Once or twice each noticed the other studying them and would smile in response.

When they had finished their meal, Sheski helped Lana clear the table. He did the job skillfully, like a man who was used to it.

Coffee was ready to be served, so Lana invited her date into the living room.

Sheski took off his dark sport coat and placed it neatly on one of the chairs. His Glock, which he now always carried with him, was nestled in a holster at the waist of his white shirt, just above his right kidney. He deftly removed his weapon and its holder, placing them on top of his coat.

Lana glanced at the firearm and back at her date. She hated guns, but understood his need to carry one at all times.

The couple sat on the burgundy couch facing the gas fireplace insert, which Lana turned on with a remote control. The fake logs glowed like a real fire, only without the smoke and mess. It was mesmerizing to them both.

After a few minutes, the lieutenant turned toward Lana and pulled her close. He nuzzled her sweet-smelling hair and tilted her face up to his. The kiss was gentle at first and then became forceful. When he finally pulled himself away, they were both breathing heavily. Lana had actually swooned from the heady emotions evoked by the kiss, and took a minute to regain her composure.

It was at that instant that Bunky began to growl, which grew into a full bark. Lana jumped up off the couch, crying, "He never growls like that, and he only barks when someone is around."

Sheski was swiftly out of his seat right behind her, gun in hand.

When they got to the laundry room, Bunky was up on the low window seat that Lana had strategically placed so he could see through the curtains into the yard. The small dog was alternately sniffing and viciously barking his head off at something outside. Lana raced to the kitchen, flipped the outside floodlight on and heard Sheski yell, "I think I see someone out there. You stay here." The lieutenant was out the back door before she could respond.

Lana stepped out onto the brick patio to observe what was happening. She could barely see his form sweeping professionally through the yard and around the outbuildings. She shivered in the night air, straining to listen, but heard nothing. After a few minutes, she could distinguish Sheski's outline as he made his way noiselessly around the side of the house from the front walk. His gun was at his side. A definite skunk odor was in the air.

"Oh my gosh," Lana cried. "It's a skunk." She quickly closed the door behind her date and started to laugh. He managed a laugh with her. He smelled the animal, too, but knew that was no skunk that he saw running from behind the carriage house. Starting tonight, this property would be under surveillance . . . with or without her approval.

He wondered why anyone would be watching Lana's house. Was it connected to the murder? What did they think she knew? Or had? Maybe Lana saw or heard something that could identify the killer and didn't know it. After all, she was the first one on the scene. He kept his thoughts to himself, not wanting to frighten her with his suspicions. He made a mental note to check in at the office and get someone assigned to this place tonight.

"I should be going," he said reluctantly. "I have a very early day tomorrow. Thank you again for dinner and our time together. I really enjoyed it. Next time, I'll cook for you."

"I had a good time too, Tommy. Really. I hope we can do it again."

"Count on it," he said softly, grinning at her.

Lana got his coat off the rocker in the library, handed it to her date, and walked with him to the front door.

"Be sure and keep all the doors locked," he said while putting his coat on.

Ready to go, Tommy leaned against the front door and gently pulled her close to him in a loving embrace. "And be careful," he said tenderly.

Lana relaxed against his strong arms and could feel

his heart beating through his overcoat. "I will," she replied faintly. They exchanged telephone numbers and he promised to call her the next day. After a long embrace and a good-bye kiss, they parted.

Minutes later, after a phone call from the lieutenant, a plain-clothes state policemen was on his way to guard Lana.

Chapter Thirteen

Lieutenants Sheski and James arrived at the Danville area at 7 A.M. This was going to be a long day for them. They had several interviews to do. They had been trying to get Jess Walter to come in to talk to them, but he was not answering his phone. If they were unsuccessful today at reaching him, they would go to his home.

Rose's funeral was to start at 11A.M. The detectives were not invited, but were going anyway. They planned on attending after getting coffee at The Bridge Stop diner.

Sheski was beginning to feel like a regular there, as the friendly staff were greeting him by name now. He and Mike drank the Jamaican blend, with Sheski craning his neck to observe customers when they came through the front door.

"Who are you looking for?" Mike teased with a smile, knowing full well who his friend had in mind.

Sheski told his friend about his date with Lana and the interest he had in seeing her again.

Mike became solemn. "It's about time you got back into circulation again. I know you've had a rough time of it." He added, "Lana seems like a nice person— pretty, too. Keep me posted on any developments."

Mike thought about his own wife, Lillian, and how after sixteen years, he still loved her deeply. He couldn't imagine losing her. His partnership with Sheski had started shortly before Lois's death. It was long enough, though, to recognize true love when he saw it. So many of their fellow staties had bad marriages or poor relationships due to the demands of the job. Many times he and Sheski had remarked on how lucky they were. Then that awful phone call came, with Sheski wailing and in shock. It was several years before his friend could even start to date again. He and Lillian had even tried fixing him up with a cousin one time. It didn't take. Mike hoped that maybe this would be different.

After coffee, the two lieutenants spent the early morning interviewing Barry Brown's customers. There were six regular patrons of Zimmerman's Gardening Service, including Dr. Burns, for whom Barry worked. All were wealthy. The first five told similar stories. Barry always arrived on time, kept to himself, spoke little, and did a magnificent job. He easily outworked men ten years younger. And he had a green thumb when it came to their precious plants and shrubbery.

Upon glimpsing their yards, the lieutenants couldn't deny it. Each of the properties was beautifully maintained. The trees and shrubs were all sculpted as if drawn with colored pencils. There wasn't a leaf or petal out of place. Borders and edgings were meticulously spaced and planted. How he managed that was anyone's guess. He didn't carry a ruler or level with him; it was all done with the eye. He was obsessed with perfection, and it paid off. Barry even mixed his own plant fertilizers, closely guarding the formula. When his boss asked him for it, Barry grimly and silently shook his large, shaggy head back and forth. He wasn't sharing. His patrons paid plenty for his services, but they didn't begrudge it. Zimmerman's had a goldmine in Barry, they observed. Further, they all tipped Barry well, out of fear of losing him to someone else. There was a long waiting list of locals who wanted to woo the gardener away from the regulars. When the lieutenants asked, none of his customers knew where the missing man might be, and none believed him capable of murder. He was too quiet and too shy, they agreed. They all wanted him found safe and sound. After all, their properties would not be the same without him.

The customers had noted, though, that in the past few months, Barry was having some difficulties. He was moving much more slowly and experiencing problems with anything heavy. They thought that whatever it was would pass. They were willing to wait him out. That's how good he was. Sheski noted on his pad to check with Barry's physician.

Mike kept a watch on the time and when it was getting to be midmorning, he drove the unmarked state police car to the funeral home. Although the investigators involved in this case were not formally invited, these two would be there anyway. Some of their best investigation results emerged from attending services such as these. Surprisingly, many killers attended their victim's interment. They seemed to get some kind of secondary gratification out of the service, burial, and responses of the family and friends to their loved one's demise.

Sheski had donned his dark suit, white shirt, and plain dark tie for the early morning service. Mike was dressed similarly. They arrived at the funeral home at 10 A.M., an hour early, the first non-family members there.

Neither lieutenant was fond of this part of their job. Most times, in the interest of the investigation, they were able to put their personal feelings aside. Today was no different. They easily found the place, a large brick house converted into a funeral home, as are many big old homes in this part of the country.

Upon entering the foyer, they were greeted by the funeral director, a distinguished-looking man in his seventies, who quietly took their coats and showed them to the guest register, where they signed their names. Only three names were ahead of theirs. The registry showed the signatures of Dr. Lesley Stone, husband, Karen Stone, daughter, and Ruth Wagner, cousin of the deceased. Outside, cars were beginning to park on the street, with black-clothed occupants preparing to pay their respects.

Rose's closed casket rested on a bier against a back wall in what appeared to once have been an immense parlor. It was a magnificent walnut casket, hand-engraved with rose bouquets. Brass hardware added an elegant touch. Draping the top of the casket was a garland of pink and white roses that cascaded down over the side and hung nearly to the floor. A red ribbon declared in gold letters, *Beloved Wife.* To the left of the garland, at the very head of the coffin, lay a small bouquet of white rosebuds with feathery fern accents. Dangling from the flowers was a small white ribbon with the word *Mother* in dainty gold script. The effect gave the false impression of a much-adored family member.

Flanking the casket were dozens of floral tributes in containers of various shapes and sizes. Most were in the upper-spending bracket that must have kept florists in the area busily preparing for hours. Strategically-placed signed cards identified the senders.

Heavy, dark green drapes outlined bay windows on the east wall. A parquet oak floor gave testament to a time when Pennsylvania was the lumber capital of the world and hardwoods were generously used. A pink Aubusson carpet covered the center of the floor, and low-backed velvet chairs lined the first row for grieving family members. Behind them, like stark witnesses to bereavement and mourning, were row after row of wooden folding chairs. Including an overflow area, there was seating for at least a hundred.

Sheski peered from the hallway into the viewing room to see Dr. Stone standing near the head of the casket, talking intimately with a middle-aged, heavy-set woman. Sheski deduced correctly that the grieving female, dressed in a dark polyester dress and black flats, was Rose's only cousin, Ruth Wagner from Toledo. She had not seen her only cousin in more than a year, not because of any conflict, but due to their individual heavy schedules. Ruth had a great deal in common with Rose and they supported each other in their endeavors.

The owner of her own construction business, Ruth was a real go-getter, used to pushing people around to get what she wanted. Back in Toledo, she had about as many friends as Rose could claim in Danville. Both women were bullies and got lip service of loyalty and friendship but, behind their backs, most people just wished they would go away. In a manner of speaking, Rose did.

From the hallway near the guest book where the detectives were standing, it appeared that Ruth and Lesley were having a disagreement. They were talking and gesturing, unaware of the lieutenants' presence. Lips firmly set in a grim expression, Ruth seemed to want something and, whatever it was, Lesley was not giving it up. Occasionally, the lieutenants could hear a word or two and, in the heat of the discussion, the voices became loud enough that they understood what Ruth was after. She was trying to coerce the doctor into giving her the famous Darling Diamond. Her not-so-persuasive argument was that Rose had promised it to her as her only other relative. After all, weren't they like sisters? Ruth argued.

Apparently Dr. Stone was having none of it. He set his own jaw firmly, telling Ruth to forget it, the diamond was his and his alone. And when it was found, he concluded, she was not getting it. With that, he defiantly turned his back to her and stared down at the coffin.

Karen Stone, dressed in a black suit and low heels, was sitting on a chair in the front row of mourners. Sheski couldn't help but notice that she had nice legs. *Not as nice as Lana's,* he thought. Conspicuously absent was Jess Walter. Karen looked lost without him and had her head bowed as if in prayer. In her hands was a paper that appeared to be the funeral program.

While Mike stayed back near the registry, Sheski quietly approached Karen, and told her again how sorry he was about her mother. He then sat down in an adjoining chair to make conversation with her easier. Karen explained to him that Jess had wanted to escort her through the difficult day's events, to be supportive, but he still was not feeling well. And, in the interest of keeping what little peace there was in the family, he'd decided to stay home. She was sorry now to have given in to those pressures, because she really needed him.

Sheski spoke words of understanding and felt sorry for Karen's predicament. She had noticeable circles under her eyes and her pretty face was showing signs of strain. Karen thanked him for coming and then, once again, bowed her head. Sheski joined Mike at the back of the room.

Dr. Stone, still at the head of the coffin, got a glimpse of Sheski out of the corner of his eye and was not pleased to see that he was talking to his daughter. Stone was uncertain how much the lieutenant had seen the night before when he and Kylie were together in the library of his home. After Sheski had left, he worried that the policeman was too smart for his own good. It made him uncomfortable that the two staties were at the viewing.

Dr. Stone walked over to Karen, said something into her ear, and approached the lieutenants in the hallway. The two men saw him coming and held their ground. "Is this standard procedure, attending the funeral of someone whose murder you are investigating?" Stone asked.

Mike indicated that they frequently did so out of respect for the deceased.

The psychiatrist's eyes narrowed and he said stonily, "Like hell. You investigators are like vultures. Just hanging around trying to gather something that you can use against innocent people."

His harsh tone surprised the two men. They were used to the behaviors of myriad suspects, but most kept an air of civility between themselves and the police. He was no ordinary suspect. They knew it and so did he. Dr. Stone was cracking a little.

The staties moved to the side of the room, blending in with others who were waiting to talk to Rose's family.

Attending the service were about a hundred local friends and acquaintances. The place was full. Some came out of respect for the family. Others, not sorry to bid a troublemaker goodbye, came out of curiosity.

Rose had been on many community boards, including her favorite, the Restoration Committee, and many of those groups were represented today. When Sheski looked about the crowd for familiar faces, he noticed Richard and Kylie Burns entering through the front door just ahead of Sarah Grove and the two women with whom he had seen her at Stone Haven. He wondered who was minding the office.

The Burnses made their way to pay their respects to Lesley and Karen, who appeared to have called a truce for the occasion. Richard went first, shook Lesley's hand, and hugged Karen. Tears flowed down the grieving daughter's cheeks as she accepted his warm words.

Kylie held Karen's hand and drew her close in a half-hug, expressing her sorrow. Kylie then fully embraced Lesley, whispering in his ear.

A line of sympathizers was beginning to form and the investigators noticed more familiar faces. Gordon and Gladys Ashman warmly hugged and consoled the Stones before making their way to Rose's bier. They were sorrowful and held onto each other as they said their silent goodbyes. Attorney Smithson was talking shop with the folks in front and in back of him in the line of those waiting to pass by the casket. He distributed a few business cards to potential clients without shame, occasionally pumping hands. He also managed to keep one eye on Lesley and the other on the lieutenants.

Evan Haynes was in line, too, and Sheski saw Jerry pressuring him again about the divorce case they were working on. Evan peered back at Sheski with the look of a man who had had enough. Sheski smiled and shook his head in sympathy.

The line of mourners was peppered with local people the policemen recognized from downtown businesses. Sheski was busy scanning the crowd when Mike tugged lightly at his right sleeve.

Turning his head in the direction of Mike's gaze, he

saw the object of his attention. Entering the room was John Deadly. He was dressed in a dark pin-striped suit with a blue shirt and dark tie, and the tam was back on his head. *Too late,* thought Sheski, *I already saw what you're trying to hide.*

Deadly stopped directly in front of the door and was greeted by the kindly funeral director. They shook hands and he moved toward the guest book. He cast a critical glance at the floral tributes nearby and then noticed a young woman who was holding an infant over her shoulder. Deadly smiled as he gazed upon the new-born's angelic face. Entranced, he stepped closer and gently placed his large hand on the baby's soft head as he passed by, causing the child to whimper. The moth-er, unaware of the security man's touch, lovingly brought the child to her breast, comforting her.

When Deadly reached Dr. Stone, he leaned close to whisper, causing his suit coat to open. His clump of keys dangled freely from the front of his suitpants.

Sheski thought, *He must wear that thing everywhere.*

At precisely 11 A.M., the funeral service began, led by Reverend Marcus Conley, a local minister. He opened the service by stating that, at the request of the Stones, only immediate family members were invited to the gravesite following the service.

Sheski caught sight of Rose's daughter fingering the miniature Darling Diamond and crying mutely. Dr. Stone was expressionless.

Reverend Conley finished by reciting "Crossing the Bar" from a worn copy tucked inside his black King James bible. When the final Tennysonian lines were spoken, Sheski looked back to see Deadly making his way out of the door. The lieutenant guessed who Deadly's "pilot" was.

Following the short service, those in attendance left the funeral home for their cars. The remaining small procession entered waiting vehicles and the cortege crossed the river bridge. They went slowly up the hill to the Kase Cemetery where several generations of Stones were resting in graves marked with slate and marble. The black Cadillac hearse carried the coffin. Dr. Stone, Karen, and Ruth followed in an identical funeral home vehicle. Behind them in a dark blue Cadillac was Deadly, followed by Reverend Conley in his Honda Accord. Sheski and Mike were in a state car a discreet distance behind the pastor.

Getting in and out of the old cemetery would prove to be difficult because of the narrow dirt road leading through an even narrower entrance. Mike knew this, so he parked a half-mile down the road in a vacant lot and the two men walked quickly to the burial spot.

Kase was an old cemetery dating back to the nineteenth century and was not constructed with modern transport in mind. Most hearses had difficulty getting through the iron gates, and funeral directors complained endlessly to the cemetery council. The council stood firm. The old gates had been in place for more than a hundred years, and they were not about to change them now. No matter, because most people believed that with the condition the iron gates were in now, they would soon fall down on their own.

When the policemen arrived on foot, vehicles were already attempting to negotiate the tight entrance. They made it through after careful maneuvering. Reverend Conley parked next to Deadly's car, just inside the graveyard oh the side of the dirt road. The hearse pulled up further, next to the gravesite. Family members got out of the next car and walked through newly-raked grass to a small vinyl shade covering the open plot. Kase gravediggers unloaded the casket and placed it on a frame over the freshly dug hole. They then positioned themselves discreetly in a fencerow of maples and oaks just south of the cemetery.

There were three chairs, soon occupied by Ruth, Lesley, and Karen, placed in front of the walnut box. The stainless steel vault was in the ground. Its cover was resting out of sight near the back of the cemetery, awaiting placement when the last mourner paid their final farewell and departed.

The minister stood next to Karen, holding her shaking hand solemnly in his. His left arm was around her small shoulders. John Deadly remained standing behind the chairs, quietly observing the small gathering.

Sheski and Mike chose to stay out from under the tented area, leaning on large oak trees near the gravediggers. Not wanting to intrude, they remained silent and observed the final step of the interment.

Reverend Conley proceeded to the front of the casket and said a few kindly words. He shuffled off to the side, nodding for the family to come forward. Sheski's mind started to wander and he thought of Robert

Southey's description of the grave as "the threshold of eternity." *How appropriate,* he thought. *Rose, who loved restoring old buildings, has stepped upon her threshold.*

Ruth stood shaking her head back and forth solemnly as she gazed upon what was in front of her. Without so much as a word or a backward glance, she moved out from the tent toward her car, choosing her steps carefully in the soft grass so as not to twist an ankle. Her thoughts were on the diamond. Lesley and Karen were now the only ones seated in front of the grave. Deadly had not moved from directly behind them.

Suddenly Sheski became aware that something significant was about to take place. The hair stood up at the nape of his neck and he began nervously to look about. He nudged Mike, who also discerned a change in the air. The lieutenants' senses sharpened as they observed Lesley stand and place a single white rose on the hand-carved box containing his dead wife. The doctor paused a moment and took a step to the left, and waited for his daughter to come forth. Slowly Karen stood, nervously manipulating the mini Darling Diamond on her right pinky finger.

What occurred next happened so quickly that the detectives almost missed it. Karen smoothly took the ring off her hand, murmured something about being free, words that were meant to be between a daughter and her mother, and flung the diamond ring into the open grave.

Dr. Stone's face became crimson with rage as he caught sight of the valuable piece of jewelry tumbling over and over, ricocheting off the brass casket trim until it was no longer visible in the soft dirt below. He futilely lunged forward as if to stop its descent, screaming, "My God, Karen, are you out of your mind? That ring was worth a bundle." Stone then grabbed his daughter's shoulders in his hands and pulled her frightened face close to his. She began to cry. Her father continued shaking her savagely before remembering there were witnesses to his violent outburst. He loosened his grip. During this explosion, Deadly had moved threateningly closer behind Karen. He pushed himself against her back, his hot breath upon her right ear, and breathed words that only Karen could hear. The young woman was pinned helplessly against her mother's coffin.

"Let me alone. I'm free from all of you, finally, free," Karen screamed while attempting to wrest herself loose. Reverend Conley's eyes widened and before he could move, Mike was in the fray, liberating her from the attackers. His rapid intervention surprised everyone except his partner. Karen, who was now safely behind him, began sobbing openly. Sheski stood firmly by Mike's side, both policemen poised with their hands in front of them, ready should the other men try anything further.

Dr. Stone tried to apologize to the stunned observers, claiming, "I don't know what came over me. I'm sorry, I'm just not myself these days."

He then turned on his heels and practically ran toward the Cadillac. Orders were flung at the driver and the car backed quickly out of the cemetery. Before those remaining could speak, Deadly, too, was in his car and gone.

"Are you okay?" the Reverend asked of Karen worriedly.

"I'm fine." She rubbed her right kidney area lightly. "I'll be all right." Her eye make-up was smudged on her face and tears coursed down both cheeks. "I'm glad I did it. That ring was a symbol of something that never really existed. They never loved me. Never," she said sadly. "My mother only loved her possessions and her committees. And Father, well, Father only loves money." Karen realized that she had never admitted that to herself until this moment. She started to feel a little dizzy. "I need to sit down," she said. Reverend Conley assisted her to a chair.

"Are you sure that you want that ring to be buried with your mother?" Sheski asked.

"Yes, I'm sure," she said determinedly. "And I'm staying right here until the last shovelful is on to make sure it's not removed." *And when the sun rises tomorrow,* Karen thought, *Jess and I will begin making wedding plans. It's time I took control of my own life.*

"I'll stay with you," Reverend Conley said comfortingly. "When you're ready to leave, I can take you home."

Sheski and Mike started walking away from the cemetery toward their car. Neither thought that Karen's attackers would return. The men looked back in time to see that the gravediggers had lowered the coffin into the dark earth. Soon, clumps of earth were deposited over the casket and ring. Karen and the Reverend stayed, as she had vowed, until the last of the dark, moist dirt was in place.

Chapter Fourteen

Lying on his side in the grass near a back entrance, Oliver Pratt hoisted himself onto one elbow. Lunch was finished and there was some time to write and paint before evening chores. He was glad that it was an unusually warm November. His child was due to be born soon and he was hoping the infant's mother would not have to be cold during the delivery.

Carefully, while looking around to make sure no one could see him, he pulled his journal out from under a white long-sleeved shirt, opened the pages, and began to write.

"November fourth, 1937. All of the cattle were fed by five A.M. today. Fortunately, it was a good harvest this year and we will have enough grain and hay to take us into next summer. I don't mind my barn chores. We all must do our part to contribute to the hospital community. The care of the cows is easy and the milking keeps these sore hands supple. For an old painter like myself, that is a blessing. I am old but will not get much older. I do not think that I will see another spring. I feel myself slowing down. What a pity. What a waste. Most of my life spent in the confines of this pathetic excuse for a mental ward. Thankfully, my father's money buys me plenty of canvasses, paints, and freedom. But I could have done so much more. And the paintings that I could have completed . . ." He put his pencil down.

Oliver pulled back the pages from earlier months' writings and read the scrawling words that outlined his days. He enjoyed reading about the times that provided him with pleasure and joy. His particular favorites were the early years in Philadelphia and the more recent times he spent here with his Becky. He read a particular favorite:

We have been able to secure some time together almost daily in my room for a few well-placed dollars. Becky is frequently melancholy but is always willing to do what I ask. She is a skillful seamstress and makes herself garments designed to make her look like a young child. It is a poor substitute, but is the best I can do in here. She doesn't seem to completely grasp the encounters that we reenact together. No matter. I love her for giving this old man a chance to relive some glorious moments.

The ever-present grin reappeared as he read each delicious line. He pictured the depressed Becky in little-girl dresses, talking as a six-year-old would, playing with her dolly. He could make her do anything he wanted, just as he did with the others. And he didn't have to hurt her afterward to protect himself from being discovered. She had a flair for the arts and understood his instruction about light and perspectives much more than the little ones. And she didn't cry when they had sex in return for his lessons.

Feeling invigorated, he closed the calfskin cover over the pages, got up, and slowly walked the pathway back to his room to paint.

Chapter Fifteen

Rose's funeral filled their morning and part of the afternoon. It was now later in the day, and the lieutenants had an appointment with Richard and Kylie Burns at their home on Mill Street. This would make for a long day, but they did not want to miss the opportunity to interview Dr. and Mrs. Richard Burns. Since they were already so close to their home, the only Victorian house on Danville's main street, they chose to speak to the Burnses there. Nestled among glass storefronts and businesses, this would be the lieutenants' last stop on the list of Barry Brown's customers.

Richard's mother, Rebekah, had lived in this home also. She left it upon suffering from post-partum depression after her first child was stillborn. Unable to recover without inpatient help, she spent several years in the psychiatric unit of the now-defunct Danville Medical Hospital. Rumor had it that she and the infamous Oliver Pratt had struck up a close friendship, spending long hours together before his death—a rumor the Burns family denied. Nine years after her discharge from the facility, her son Richard was born.

The policemen had called ahead, so the psychiatrist knew they were coming. He warned them he could not spare much time.

They were right on time. As they approached the Second Empire structure, the lieutenants stopped to collect their thoughts.

"Hey, Sheski," Mike queried, "How much do you think a place like this would cost?"

"More than you and I together will ever see," he replied.

Sheski looked up at the multi-colored slate, Mansard-style roof protecting paneled freeze-boards and dormer windows, wondering how a person kept a place like this in such immaculate condition.

Authentic Victorian colors were painted on slender Pennsylvania pine siding. A cresting on the roof topped off the rich, colorful structure. The house was set close to Mill Street, separated by a few feet of Barry Brown-manicured yard and a low decorative iron fence. The effect was one of elegance and charm.

When Sheski reached for the doorbell, his hand brushed across a bronze plaque fastened to the side of the double doors. Peering closer, he read:

"THIS PROPERTY HAS BEEN PLACED ON THE NATIONAL REGISTER OF HISTORIC PLACES BY THE UNITED STATES DEPARTMENT OF THE INTERIOR."

Impressive, he thought.

Kylie Burns opened the door for them, dressed in tailored brown slacks and matching jacket over a cream colored blouse open at the neck. A single gold chain with a large diamond hugged her throat.

"Please come in," she said coolly, stepping aside for the men. She eyed Sheski in particular, wondering just how much he had seen in the Stones' library the night of Rose's death. The policeman's expression was noncommittal.

In the background, they could hear several dogs barking.

"They won't hurt you," Kylie stated fondly. "They're such sweet babies. They wouldn't hurt anyone."

They entered a twelve-foot wide foyer with an open staircase that continued up three floors, and were ushered through pocket doors into a drawing room. It was furnished with a scarlet oriental rug and period furnishings that looked like an illustration out of *Godey's Lady's Book.* She motioned for them to sit down and said she would inform her husband they had guests.

Unexpectedly, four dogs of various sizes and breeds rushed in to greet the guests. Two border collies, a Yorkshire Terrier like Lana's, only bigger, and a mixed-breed completed the ensemble. The meticulously groomed pets wagged their tails and made every effort to get to know their new visitors.

"Alright, you nosy little honeys," Kylie said in a motherly tone to the dogs. She petted each one, taking care to give individual attention to them all. The dogs, accustomed to such affection, followed their mistress around, all vying for her notice.

Kylie's face brightened as she looked fondly at her charges. "Richard and I have no children, so these are my babies," she explained. "I saved two of them from the dog pound and the others were strays that were found wandering around town. It's horrible how some people treat their animals, leaving them to get hurt or starve. We have many abandoned dogs and cats at the shelter right now." She got an idea and said, "Are either of you two looking for a pet? There're some really adorable dogs down there."

The lieutenants assured her they weren't presently looking for a pet, but would keep it in mind.

Kylie smiled at their response and left the room to get her husband. Her four charges followed, the mutt pushing closest to his benefactress.

The policemen surveyed the antiques before choosing a place to sit. Sheski lowered his large frame onto an uncomfortable Eastlake needlepoint-covered side chair while Mike sat gingerly on a small antique corner seat. Out of view of their hosts, they threw each other glances that expressed the impossibility of finding anything in that room suitable to sit on. They figured that Kylie's placement of them in this setting may have been intentional.

Dr. Richard Burns entered the drawing room with the air of an important man who had places to be and people to see. His well-groomed, moderate-length blond hair hung about an inch over his ears and down over his collar in the back. It looked like a hairstyle he might have had in college and had never changed. Small, round glasses were perched on his nose. The doctor's wife followed behind him, this time without the dogs.

Both lieutenants rose to shake hands with the dark-suited man. Sheski stared him full in the face, turned away, and then looked beyond the John Lennon tinted glasses into his eyes. There was something compelling about the doctor's gaze. Sheski introduced himself and Mike while the host and hostess settled into matching side chairs for their interview.

"I hope my wife's pets didn't annoy you too much," the doctor began. "That's her passion in life, you see. She single-handedly supports the financing of the local dog shelter and volunteers there two days a week. She'd have ten dogs in this house if I'd permit it. Which I don't. Four is our limit"

Kylie beamed over at her husband.

Sheski listened patiently, and then lost no time in explaining the purpose of their visit. He inquired about the doctor's whereabouts at the time of Mrs. Stone's murder.

"I knew you would want to know that, so I consulted my calendar earlier today. It seems I was conducting a session with one of my clients at the time of Rose's death. I cannot tell you the person's name but you may speak with Sarah, our secretary, to confirm my story."

Same song and dance as Dr. Stone, thought Sheski. *I've got to get to Sarah before the day is over to check these stories.*

"Dr. Burns, are you or your wife aware of anyone who would want to murder Mrs. Stone?" asked Mike concernedly. "Someone who would want to mutilate her body in such a vicious way?"

Mike kept his eyes on the doctor while Sheski was watching Kylie. She was a pretty cool lady, looking at her husband while waiting for his answer. Only the nervous clasping, unclasping of the diamond watch on her tiny left wrist betrayed the underlying anxiety that she was experiencing.

"For God's sake, Kylie, stop that," hissed her frowning husband while looking in her direction.

His remark caught her off-guard and, red faced, she stammered, "Oh, sorry, I didn't realize what I was doing."

"What was your question again?" the doctor asked Mike.

Mike repeated his question.

The Burnses simultaneously denied knowing any such person. The doctor cautiously stated that he didn't believe Mrs. Stone had any enemies, while his wife continued to deny knowing anyone who would hurt Rose.

"Rose and I have been friends a long time," Kylie stated. "We golfed together and attended each other's parties. Our husbands worked closely at Stone Haven, so we had plenty of opportunities to get together." She narrated a story of a friendly relationship that existed between the Stone and the Burns families, dating back many years.

When she finished, Sheski asked her matter-of-factly, "Where were you at the time of the murder?"

"I was at Stone Haven, waiting to see Richard."

Dr. Burns's head spun around as if in disbelief. "This

is the first I've heard of this. You knew I was with patients all day, Kylie. What did you want?"

Kylie shifted uncomfortably and crisply said, "I don't remember now, I just know that I was there. You can ask John Deadly. He saw me." She turned her gaze from his. She knew that the investigators would check her story and that Deadly would corroborate what she'd said.

Richard was eyeing his wife suspiciously. It was observed by the detectives.

Sheski wrote notes on a small pad while they finished up the interview. On their way out the door, he and Mike thanked the Burnses. Kylie was glaring at all of them when she closed the massive doors on their backs.

"If I didn't know better, I would think her husband was caught off-guard there," said Mike evenly.

Sheski began to fill his friend in on his observations of the night before. How he saw Dr. Stone and Kylie in a semi-clinch, sharing murmurings in the library.

"And his wife's body's not yet cold," snapped Mike. "A guy could get cynical on this job."

"Let's eat something and then go back to Stone Haven. I'd like to talk to the staff again. Especially the receptionist, Sarah," Sheski said.

After the special at a Mill Street restaurant, their ride to Stone Haven took just a few minutes. Again they parked their car out front and went into the imposing structure. Sarah, the secretary/receptionist, was not at her desk. Instead, there were two other women sitting there. The lieutenants recognized them as the same two who were with Sarah at the funeral. The older one introduced herself as Vickie Sims, Stone Haven's social worker. The other, she explained, glancing at her companion, was Shannon Albright, the hospital dietician. She said that they were filling in while Sarah took a powder break.

Vickie was a slightly overweight, middle-aged married woman with shoulder-length blond hair. She was a sober but friendly person, in contrast to Shannon, who smiled a lot as she spoke.

Shannon, at thirty, was younger than her friend. She was beautiful, with long black hair, fair complexion, and a knockout figure that she maintained by instructing aerobics part-time.

The policemen introduced themselves and said they had some questions for Sarah. Shannon asked if it was about Mrs. Stone's murder and the investigators nodded their heads.

"Rose will not be missed, I'm sorry to say," the dietician said crisply. "She was one of those women who had time only for herself. She was married to one of the best-looking men around, but didn't appreciate him. He's gonna be a real catch for someone," she sighed.

"Is she mooning over the boss again?" Sarah said, grinning as she crossed the floor toward them. "She's had a crush on him since she first laid eyes on him."

"Oh, I'm harmless," Shannon grinned back. "I don't want to marry him, just be able to stare at him for the rest of my life."

Up until then, Vickie had said nothing. The social worker in her just couldn't joke about someone so soon after their death. Vickie was familiar with the death and dying process, and the realities of a job in which consoling others was a daily process took their toll. "I can't believe he's back to work so soon. But different people cope with loss in different ways," she said philosophically.

"Sarah, is there somewhere we can talk privately?" Sheski asked.

"Sure," she replied. "Dr. Stone is still at lunch. We can use his office."

Without being asked, the lieutenants handed their guns over to her and, according to policy and procedure, she locked them in the hospital vault. They then followed her down the hall to the office.

Shannon volunteered to tend the desk again until Sarah returned. When the three were out of sight, Shannon and Vickie began to speculate on what the police could want with Sarah.

"She can't be a suspect," said Vickie. "They must want to just ask her some routine questions. What could she know, anyway? She was here the day of the murder until five-thirty P.M. I know because I was here, too. And, according to the police, Rose was already dead by then."

"Maybe I'll get lucky and the tall one will want to question me privately," laughed Shannon.

"What are you two all excited about?" asked Lana, stopping at the desk. Lana was back at work at Stone Haven to handle some of the heavy nursing caseload.

"A good-looking detective and his sidekick are interviewing Sarah," said Vickie. "Shannon was just saying she'd like to get her turn with the tall one. I think he said his name was Lieutenant Sheski."

Lana's face flushed and she asked guardedly, "Where are they now?"

"In Dr. Stone's office, and I saw him first," said Shannon, grinning.

That's what you think, thought Lana. "Tell the tall, good-looking lieutenant I'll be back in my office in a half-hour and to stop by when he's finished," she said with a smile. "I'll be there until six."

With that, she headed down the west wing to the second door on the left and into her office. Closing the door behind her, she could feel her heart beat rapidly at the thought of seeing him again. She quickly glanced in the mirror to make sure she looked all right, adding some lipstick to her scant make-up. Lana then turned from side to side to get a look at her gray pants suit. Satisfied, she went back out and down the hall to her appointment with a client.

"Well . . . what's that all about?" Shannon asked when Lana was out of earshot.

Vickie just shrugged her shoulders and said she didn't know, but that this could get interesting.

Inside Dr. Stone's office, Sarah was busy answering the investigators' questions. She shared with them the close friendship that she had with Rose's daughter Karen, and Karen's pain over her parents' reaction to her love affair.

"He's a really nice guy," Sarah assured them about Jess. "I've known him for a while now, and he's always a gentleman. And he loves Karen a lot. Treats her like a queen. It's made a big difference in her life. That's more than I could say about her parents. They may have given her everything she wanted, but the price they wanted in return was too high for anyone to pay. Karen was expected to go to the college they wanted, live where they said, and date only a man they approved of. Karen was just an extension of their status in the town, and they wanted to look good. At first I thought that was why she chose Jess. You know, because he's black, and Karen knew her parents wouldn't approve. After seeing them together, I realized that she really loved him. They are very happy together. It changed Karen. She's learning consideration for others. Rose couldn't stand it. Did you know that she was going to write Karen out of her will, leaving all of her money to her favorite charities?"

Sheski nodded his head in affirmation.

"Rose was going to give all her money to her causes, not even a penny to her husband. When they had the big blowup on Valentine's Day, Rose not only gave Karen and Jess the boot, she also told her husband, in front of all of them, that she knew of his affair with Kylie Burns. Rose was on a roll. She said she wasn't stupid. Kylie was turning up at Stone Haven far too often and when she had questioned that trash, John Deadly, he had lied to protect the two of them. She said she gave Deadly a tongue-lashing he'd never forget. Said she told that worthless bastard exactly what she thought of him. That's when she hired a private detective and got the evidence she needed. Neither Karen nor her father would get a dime from her. Karen was shocked to hear her mother say such things. She thought her father would deny it, but he didn't. Karen had enough and gathered up her things to leave, saying she didn't ever want to see either of them again; that she didn't need their money. That's when Rose struck her. Karen said her mother slugged her hard with a closed fist. I guess Jess stepped in and got her out of there before it became a free-for-all. Karen called me when she got home, hysterical over her parents' behavior. Jess vowed he'd not let her be struck again. Said he'd see to it."

"Do you think Jess could have murdered Rose?" asked Mike.

"No, I don't think so. I just think he meant that Karen wouldn't be going to her parents' home again until they apologized and changed their attitude. He would have had a long time to wait before that happened. The Stones are self-centered people. They wouldn't change for anyone, not even their own daughter."

Mike then redirected Sarah to the alibis that both psychiatrists gave for where they were at the time of Rose's murder. Sarah vouched that the two of them each had a session at that time, but couldn't divulge the clients' identities.

Sheski saw that she wordlessly left the appointment book wide open where he could see the names for himself if he wanted to look while they talked. Sarah was proving to be a good contact person, he thought.

Flagrantly standing over her to get a good look at the scheduled appointments, Sheski took all the time he needed. He made a mental note that Dr. Burns had a session from 3:30 P.M. until 4:15 P.M. with someone named Jamison Albright. That name didn't ring a bell. Dr. Stone's afternoon client was another matter. Sheski silently motioned for Mike to get a look. The name jumped off the page at both of them. From 3 P.M. until five, John Deadly was receiving therapy from his boss. Sheski wondered what kind of problems Deadly was working on for two full hours. From where he stood, the guy sure had some, but two hours was a long time for a therapy session.

The lieutenants finished their questioning, thanked Sarah, and told her they might need to meet again. On their way out the door, Sheski spied the Oliver Pratt journal in the glass showcase. He turned to Sarah, and with a puzzled look, asked, "Has anyone ever read that?"

"I don't know, maybe," she replied. "Dr. Stone keeps it locked up in that glass box. He says it's too fragile to be handled. More than one art critic writing on the Pratt paintings petitioned for approval to review it, but they were always turned away. It was part of the estate when Dr. Stone's mother purchased the property. So, legally he has the right to refuse. He and Deadly have the only keys to this case."

The trio returned to the receptionist's desk as Dr. Stone came through the doors. He eyed the policemen suspiciously, looked back in the direction of his office, and asked them what they were doing there.

"Routine questioning, Doctor," Mike said gravely. "We're still conducting our investigation."

"I have nothing further to say to you unless my lawyer is present. Make an appointment with him if you want to see me again." With that, he turned and briskly went into his office.

Shannon watched the handsome psychiatrist walk away, admiration written all over her lovely face. She smiled dreamily and said nothing, waving back to them as she headed off to her office.

Vickie rolled her eyes in response to her friend's lust. "Oh, by the way," she said slyly. "Lana Stahl came by and said to tell the tall, good-looking detective that she would be in her office until six; that you were to stop by and say hello." She grinned and looked back and forth expectantly from Sheski to Mike.

Mike cracked first. "I'll go on out to the car and wait for you. Take your time."

"I won't be long," Sheski said. He followed Vickie's directions to Lana's office, knocked on the door and said, "Lana?"

"Come on in, Tommy," she said excitedly. The door closed behind him.

Well, I'll be, thought Vickie. *Wait 'til I tell Shannon.* She picked up the phone, happily dialed Shannon's office number, and chattered away.

Inside Lana's office, the two grinned at each other and Lana gave him a quick hug. She was afraid to get into a clinch too long because she still had a lot of work to do and wanted to be able to do it.

Sheski saw she had an eight into ten of someone on her desk and peeked around to see who it was. He laughed when a picture of the furry Bunky, sitting on a wagon, looked back at him.

Mike didn't have too long to wait. Sheski only stayed

fifteen minutes. Not that he didn't want to stay longer, he just didn't want to compromise Lana's job or give the office gossips any more to talk about than his short visit commanded. They promised to see each other Saturday night at Sheski's house.

"Tonight, I think we'll pay John Deadly a visit at his home," Sheski said to his partner. "I'd like to check him out away from his job. See where he lives, and how he'll react to some questions. Where do you think a guy like that lives, in the sewer?"

"Nah, he probably has an upstairs apartment in town," guessed Mike.

"If we want to deal with him tonight, let's go back to the office and plan our strategy," Mike said. "And on our way, you can tell me about your visit with Lana."

"I'm not telling you anything," Sheski said good-naturedly. "Besides, there's nothing to tell."

"You're in worse shape than I thought," Mike laughingly replied.

Chapter Sixteen

The Kramer twins, Dave and Danny, middle school students, silently made their way along the muddy banks of Mahoning Creek. They had bagged yet another school day to go fishing and didn't want anyone to see or hear them for fear they would be found out. Their morning was spent under the river bridge with six-pound test lines in the water, but nothing was biting, so they walked along the soft mud to their favorite fishing hole in the adjoining creek for the afternoon.

The boys ducked under pine boughs along the murky, shallow waterway. They carried with them their prized Shakespeare fiberglass rods. After a few minutes, a spot was chosen where they couldn't be seen from West Mahoning Street, just in case someone should come looking for them. It was a good spot, with low-hanging tree branches and a hollow in the bank where the creek made a sharp angle to enter the river.

From their vantage point, they could see anyone coming without being seen themselves. Both boys settled in, nestling their backs against the cold, hard ground, on the site of the former cinder tip.

Seventy years before, waste products from the now-defunct iron mill had been dumped all along these creek banks. At that time, the area was a favorite of the town drunks and children playing games. After the mill ceased production, trees and green eventually returned and it became a popular fishing spot for locals.

The brothers got comfortable and placed their backpacks beside Dave, who prepared their lines. They had come to do some serious fishing and wanted to get to it before they had to get home.

Identical in every way physically, the towheaded boys were opposites in personalities. Dave, loud and bossy, was a full two minutes older than his brother and was the leader, speaking for the two of them when needed. Danny was quiet and reserved.

"Want a sandwich?" Dave asked his brother.

"Yep," was the reply.

A peanut butter and jelly sandwich was unwrapped and carefully handed over.

"Here, take a soda, too. I got root beer. Your favorite."

"Okay, thanks," Danny said passively. He leaned across his brother for a soda, not wanting to disturb his rod, which had a pale line snaking down into the creek. He grasped the brown-and-silver can in his left hand, then lost his grip on it, and watched in dismay as it rolled down the bank, out of his sight. He heard it plop into the creek. He looked up at his twin.

"I'll get it," Dave offered. "You watch the rods." The young boy slowly made his way down down from their refuge to where he thought the can had rolled. A couple of times his feet skidded on some stones, but he caught himself and plugged on.

After a few minutes, when Dave didn't return, Danny decided he should go after him. He, too, went slowly down to the stream, skidding and sliding at times. As he got closer to the water, the unmistakable odor of something dead was detected, causing him to proceed with caution.

He could see his brother standing there, arms at his side, staring at something half in, half out of the creek in some brush. Whatever it was, it was long, dirty, and ragged. As he drew up next to his twin, Danny got a closer look at the object of Dave's attention. There was no mistaking it. The body of what appeared to be a man was lying facedown in the water. The limbs of the corpse were twisted at odd angles, with the left arm resting under the body. It was wearing a torn green jacket with the letters . . . *erman's* appliquéd in white on the back. The soiled garment was pulled partly up the man's torso.

When Dave sensed his twin nearby, he turned and told him not to look. At this point, Danny began to gag and vomited into the creek downstream from the body. He wiped his mouth with the sleeve on his left arm and started to cry. Dave reached out and led him away from the gruesome scene. The two of them scrambled back up the creek bank, slipping and sliding.

Fear had tightly gripped their adolescent hearts, and their precious fishing gear was abandoned as they went hastily in search of help. They wanted to be found now. For the first time in his life, Dave was really scared.

Chapter Seventeen

The state police office was quiet. Sheski and Mike were in the common room with Doug, who was manning the phones and handling walk-ins. Today, work at the barracks was pretty slow. His only real interaction with the public had been to provide directions for an elderly couple, John and Clara Lee from Connecticut. The Lees had somehow driven their motor home down the wrong exit off Route 80 and were lost. Doug got the septuagenarians coffee and carefully explained to them how to get back on the interstate so they could continue their journey. As the lost couple was going out the door, the phone rang. Politely excusing himself, Doug raced back to his desk and picked up the receiver. He watched out the window as the Lees backed out of the parking lot, listening to a fellow officer on the other line. Eyes widening, he motioned for Sheski and Mike to shut up and pay attention. When the policeman finished giving the young trooper what information he had for him, Doug thanked him and turned to the others. "It looks like our missing gardener has turned up," he said. "Some boys found him facedown in a creek in Danville."

It took Sheski and Mike thirty minutes via Route 642 to get back to Danville. They parked a couple of blocks up from the high school football field and made their way to the crime scene. They hurried past vehicles and the usual horde of curious spectators, flashing their badges to get through a barricade of police cars.

Approaching the base of the creek bank, the men saw a black-and-white with identical-looking blond boys in the back seat. A young couple, the boys' parents, were sitting one on either side of the twins. One of the boys had his right arm around the other's shoulders, and the youths looked at the lieutenants as they walked by. When Sheski looked back, he noticed that photographers were busy trying to get pictures of the camerashy youngsters. The boy being comforted lowered his head, but the other was staring boldly at the newsmen.

"Get those newshounds out of here," Sheski shouted to one of the local cops. "They're just kids. Give them a break!"

The troopers carefully ascended the bank, stood on the crest, and then descended the other side to the creek. The body was positioned near the water. It had not yet been moved from the area because the town police were initially unable to locate Dr. Anthony Rae, the coroner. He was there now and had just completed his preliminary examination. Barry Brown was on his back, having been carefully turned over by investigators. His face was starting to turn black, dull features contorting into a grotesque expression.

Sheski put a clean handkerchief up to his nose and asked the coroner, "What have you got for us, Tony?"

"The poor soul was strangled with a thin wire," he replied flatly, pointing to the ligature still dangling from Barry's neck. "Besides the deep cut along the neckline, he suffered scrapes and cuts that must have happened when the body was rolled down the creek bank from the top over there." He pointed to a spot near a tall pine tree. "Oh yes, there's some sort of bruising on the right posterior kidney area. It looks like something was pushing into his lower back about the same time he was being strangled. He's been dead and down here probably since Friday. He appears to have been killed about the same time as Rose Stone. I won't be sure until the autopsy is completed, but that's my educated guess." With that, the coroner removed latex gloves from his hands and pulled a candy bar out of his pocket. He proceeded to noisily unwrap it and take a bite. "Want some?" he asked, holding the sweet out toward the lawmen. They shook their heads no.

Sheski's relationship with the coroner went back many years and he had a lot of respect for him. They had worked together on other murders, and Tony always knew what he was talking about. He was good on the witness stand, too.

Sheski figured Barry had met his maker on Friday,

just like the coroner said, and he told Mike so. With another murder on their hands, he was starting to feel the pressure to have them solved quickly.

The men moved away from the body and climbed to the top of the creek bank. Being careful not to lose their balance, the detectives and the coroner descended the slippery knoll to a grassy area below, where they paused to catch their breath.

"By the way, guys," the coroner said. "I finished the autopsy on Mrs. Stone. There was no sign of sexual intercourse or sexual assault, so we can rule out rape. One other thing—she had the same peculiar bruise on her back that I found on Barry. On her it was up a little higher, but it appears that whatever was gouging into Barry's kidneys got Mrs. Stone's right mid-scapula. I think our killer has two victims. The media's gonna love this." He finished off his candy bar and pulled out another one. Unwrapping it, he happily took a bite and started chewing.

The words no sooner left his mouth when a smiling Terry Ryder, pad and pencil poised, approached the men and asked, "What's going on here, guys? What can you give me?"

Sheski found Terry to be the least pushy of the local newspaper reporters.

"Nothing right now," he replied. "Go wait by your van, Terry, and we'll give you a statement in a couple of minutes."

"Aw, come on, I don't have all day," he whined. "I have a deadline, you know."

"We won't be long," Mike added.

"Okay," the reporter replied grudgingly. Walking away, he shot back, "But don't forget where I am."

The troopers waited for him to get out of earshot before they resumed their conversation.

"Looks like this eliminates Barry Brown as a suspect in the Stone murder," Mike said to his buddy.

Mike furrowed his eyebrows. "But Lana said she saw the gardener before she went in the house and found Rose."

"She must have been mistaken. Maybe it was someone else other than Barry that Lana saw out there in the yard holding a gardening tool. Maybe what she really saw was the murderer with the murder weapon," Sheski replied. "Barry Brown might have been murdered so the killer could get to Rose."

His eyes hardened and he said with alarm to his partner, "That's why Lana's being followed. Maybe the murderer was there when she arrived, pretending to be the gardener. He might think she can identify him."

"She might not have wanted a guard," Mike added. "But I'm glad we went ahead and placed someone with her anyway."

Sheski looked at Mike grimly and nodded. "I telephoned him not long ago to make sure he was on the job. He sounded tired but assured me there was no activity going on so far."

"Well, now," Sheski began. "With a prime suspect out of the way, we need to take a closer look at some of the others on our list. I have a hunch about the marks on the victims' backs, Mike. Let's deal with Terry and then get over to the library. There's something I want to check out in some back issues of the local newspapers before we go see Deadly."

As they started down the street to the reporter's van, one of the local policemen, Andy Wallace, called out to them. He approached the two lieutenants and said in a low voice, "Sorry to interrupt, but I have something I thought you might like to see."

He pulled a small white cotton hanky out of his pocket and gingerly opened the cloth to show them some shining items heaped together in the center. Lying regally on the clean material were dirty but expensive looking drop diamond earrings in platinum settings, pieces of sodden grass caught in their prongs. Nestled next to them were a diamond platinum watch and a necklace, the chain knotted and broken. Despite being muddy, their luster was still evident.

"These were found in Barry's pockets," the policeman said. "We think it's the jewelry that was stolen from Rose Stone's body. They match up with what her husband listed as missing."

"Beautiful," Mike said admiringly. "Top of the line."

"Is that it? No ring?" Sheski asked.

"No ring," Andy said firmly. "Dr. Stone sounded pretty upset when I called and told him what we found. He insisted we do a search of the area around the body and in the creek for the diamond ring. Made a big deal about it. Mahoning Creek sure is cold this time of the year," he digressed. "Anyway, we did what he asked and still didn't find it. He was furious when we came up empty, came real close to saying something he might have regretted later. I've known him all my life and I'm not gonna take any abuse from him. He's lucky we got what we did. It all could have floated on down into the Susquehanna." Andy rolled the jewelry over on the cloth and said, "If her ring went with the current, some lucky so-and-so may catch a bass someday and get more than a meal out of it." He chuckled at the thought. "Oh yeah, do you want to interview the twins that found the body, you two? They're still here."

"No, I'll read your report and if there's anything further I need from them, I'll call later. Poor kids. They're probably pretty shaken. Keep those photographers out of their faces and let the parents take them home."

They watched Andy march toward the police car to chase the cameras away and tell the Kramers that they could take their sons home. The photographers complained but, cameras flashing, found other subjects for their lenses.

Mike turned to his partner. "What do you make of them finding the jewelry on Barry?"

"I'm not sure. If he didn't kill Mrs. Stone, someone might want us to think it was him. Barry sure didn't tie that wire around his own neck, though."

Hearing a door slam, the lieutenants looked over at Terry, who was out of the company van, smiling and waving at them, his sleeves flapping against long, skinny arms. He was pointing at his pad and pen and then at his watch.

"Let's get this over with," Sheski said with a deep sigh. "Then we'll go to the library." He managed a half-hearted smile and they walked toward the reporter.

Chapter Eighteen

Mike parked the car on Ferry Street on the east side. "This must be the area where Dr. Stone's brother waltzed into the river," Mike said as they got out of the vehicle.

"Yes, it is," his partner replied. "I wanted to get a closer look at that scene before it gets dark. Also, there are some things I want to check in the library. Dr. Stone seems to have too many tragic deaths in his family. Most people go through life and don't even suffer one such event, but he seems to have quite a few. His brother, Samuel, drowns down there," he said, motioning towards the river. "And his mother is killed in an unfortunate car accident. I get bad vibes when one of our suspects has that kind of a history."

The two men made their way down the sloping street to the sidewalk along the river park. Carefully, they walked the stony path down to the muddy banks of the

Susquehanna. It was difficult for them to imagine anyone wanting to swim in that beautiful river, day or
night. The river had a reputation with swimmers, and
not a good one either. At least once a year a fisherman
without a life vest would drown in waters that most
people thought were shallow from shore to shore.
Swimmers of all ages and experience had drowned
there over the years, too, their bodies pulled down into
hidden pockets of deep pooling water with barely-
detectable whirlpools churned from the rapid currents.

There didn't seem to be anything new here to learn,
but Sheski wanted to take a look at it anyway. He wanted to get a feel for the area where that crazy young man
had met his death. It was a bucolic scene, the tree-
covered hills on the south side, sloping down toward
the north branch. The flowing river with the sun glint-
ing on gray-green waters was mesmerizing, and the
men had to force themselves to look away and get back
up to the library.

Sheski talked as he walked. "Most libraries keep
back issues of newspapers on microfilm. Let's go in
and see if they have them here dating back to the nine-
teen sixties. We've been over the materials in our files,
but I want to see if we can learn anything new or different from the newspapers about our locals involved in
these cases."

The two policemen rounded the corner and walked
up the stone steps and through the double doors leading
into the vestibule. They stepped onto the tile floor,
opened the second set of entry doors and entered a
building that, except for the copier under the oak open

stairwell, hadn't changed since it was built in the 1880s.

As he approached the librarian's desk, Sheski saw an oak card catalog cabinet to his right. Hand-printed directions on an index card taped to the top of the file indicated that the cabinet to the left had books catalogued by titles, and the card file on the right was catalogued by author. *This is one library that hasn't yet gone to the computer system,* he thought. Despite the extra work he knew would be involved without a computer system, he found this oddly pleasing.

Mike approached the aged librarian, identified on her name pin as Marian, and asked how they might locate old newspaper articles. She was a heavy-set, pleasant-looking woman, with her gray hair pinned back neatly in a bun.

Marian whispered an explanation that the local newspapers were filed first under the paper's name and then according to years, months, and days. If they would bring her the file number of the newspapers they wanted, she would have someone get them from storage.

"We haven't yet gone to a computer system," she apologized in a low voice. "But we're hoping to in the near future. It's so expensive, you know. So," she went on kindly, "Original papers will have to do."

Sheski thanked her and fingered through the small cards in the drawers for the items he needed. He wrote down the file numbers for newspapers of the *Danville News,* dated July 25 to July 31, 1968, and July 25–31, 1969. For further information, he also wrote numbers for another local paper, the *Morning Press,* same dates.

He took his list to the smiling Marian. She explained that it would take her some time but while she searched for the papers, they could wait in the periodicals room. She rose from her chair with a great deal of effort, kyphosis impeding her movements.

Mike led the way through doors with the word *Gentlemen* lettered in gold on the glass. A bronze plaque on the wall to the left of the doors informed the public that the room was furnished *For the citizens of Danville by Mrs. Elizabeth Hastings Stone.* A fireplace with a large mirror over the white marble mantle stood in the middle of one wall. Original stained glass windows lined the other three. The men placed themselves in oak captain's chairs and leaned on the library table. Copies of the day's newspapers hung on wooden pole racks nearby, waiting to be read.

"I guess we could read something while we wait. This might take awhile," Sheski said.

Mike agreed and the two men started rummaging through stacks of well-worn paperback novels for sale on the fifty-cent rack.

Sheski was enjoying what he was seeing and hearing. This old library, with its converted brassoliers and cast iron radiators, was like stepping back in time. He preferred this in contrast to a sterile, modern building.

After a while, his musings were interrupted by the sound of creaking wheels. Despite a spinal curvature, the librarian was happily pushing a wooden cart piled with two weeks' worth of old newspapers. Each was in a plastic sheath with an identification tag displayed prominently on the front.

"Here you go, young man. One of our volunteers got them for you. I hope you find what you're looking for. If we can be of any further help, please let me know."

Young man, Sheski thought. *I haven't been called that in a while.* It brought a smile to his face.

The librarian made a quick exit to go shush some grade school children who were across the aisle in the opposite room. What once must have been a reading room for the women was now filled with children's books and child-sized tables and chairs. Upon seeing the aged librarian, the source of the whispers became silent. Marian then made her way back to the librarian's desk to assist a young couple who had placed their library card and several bestsellers on the counter.

Sheski and Mike sat back down on the captain's chairs at a long oak table with lion's feet supports. They spread the newspapers out on the tabletop with the *Morning Press* papers going to Mike, and Sheski keeping the *Danville News.* They began the task of trying to find press releases on the events surrounding the deaths of Samuel and Elizabeth Stone.

Sheski had been told by Andy Wallace that each of their accidents had taken place in the last week of July, one year apart, but was uncertain about the exact dates.

"Check each newspaper until we have both the headlines and any follow-up articles, including the obituaries. See if there are any other interesting articles about these people that would help us get a better picture of them," he said quietly to Mike. "I have a hunch I want to follow."

The two men pored over their early editions of the

local newspapers, stopping every now and then to mention something that struck them as unusual or amusing.

"Check this out," cried Mike. "Admission to the Capitol Theater is one dollar and a loaf of bread at the A & P costs forty-nine cents."

His partner laughed and said, "Keep reading; that's not what I'm looking for."

The July 28, 1968, news narratives of the death of Mrs. Elizabeth Hastings Stone were similar in both papers.

Sheski read aloud. " 'She was en route about eight P.M. July twenty-seventh, to her decorator's place of business in Catawissa via a convoluted country road when the accident took place. The dangerous unlit route follows the railroad tracks next to the river. The state police believe that a dog or some other creature ran out in front of Mrs. Stone's Rolls Royce, causing her to swerve to avoid striking it. Skid marks one hundred feet long were noted near the scene. Mrs. Stone lost control of the light blue luxury car at a point where there are no guardrails and went over the fifty-foot drop to the train tracks below. Death followed quickly. There were no eyewitnesses and, because of the sparsely-populated area, the crash went unreported until the next morning, when the wreckage was spotted by a passer-by driving to work.' "

To the right of the article was a picture of the middle-aged Mrs. Stone. It showed a smiling, very attractive, light-haired woman. The *Danville News* quoted several prominent citizens who spoke glowingly of her philanthropical activities and her generosity to those in need. Reverend Joseph Henry of the Methodist Church, her pastor, told of the many missionaries she supported. The July 28 obituary acknowledged Mrs. Stone's community activities and the many charities that she supported. There was also a brief mention of a community foundation that she was putting together prior to her death. It was to have been supported by the Stone estate, the article noted, but sadly was unfinished and subsequently died with her.

"She was quite a woman," Mike commented. "Nice-looking, too. Dr. Stone resembles her a little, don't you think?"

Sheski studied the picture closely. "Only in looks," he said sarcastically. "She sounds like a caring human being. What a loss."

The detectives continued their review of the newspapers for accounts of Samuel's death. After about thirty minutes, Sheski found himself engrossed in an extensive front-page news article. When he finished, he let out a loud whistle and said excitedly to Mike, "Will you look at this!" Sheski was pointing to a headline of the *Danville News,* July 29, 1969, which proclaimed, "Local Man Feared Dead in River." Subcaption: "Eyewitness tells of Mental Patient's Plunge into the Susquehanna."

Sheski quietly read to Mike the first paragraph of a lengthy story. " 'John Deadly, on a two-week leave from the army, contacted the Danville Police at eleven-fifteen P.M. last evening to report witnessing a young man, Samuel Stone, running into the river. According to Mr. Deadly, a Danville native, he couldn't sleep last night so decided to take a walk along the river to relax. He had just sat down on one of the park benches to rest when he heard a commotion at the junction of Front and Ferry Streets. Looking up to see where it was coming from, he reported that he saw nineteen-year-old Samuel Stone talking to himself and gesturing wildly while running naked down Ferry Street in the direction of the river. Before he had a chance to stop him, the young man dashed down a lane leading to the water and ran into the shallow waterway.' "

Sheski read on. " 'Mr. Deadly reported chasing after Samuel but, sadly, was unable to intercept him before it was too late. The young man swam out into the deeper section of the river, doggie-paddled for a while and then went under several times before disappearing from view in the strong undercurrent. Area police, well aware of the dangerous flow of dark water, fear the worst.' "

Mike read the remainder of the article over Sheski's shoulder. The story documented Samuel Stone's previous history of manic depression and his treatment with the new drug Lithium. It also reported that he was often noncompliant with a medication regimen that, for efficacy, required strict adherence by the patient. The newspaper quoted Samuel's brother, Lesley, a student at Harvard, as saying he knew that his only sibling was recently fighting a bout of mania. Lesley Stone further said that he had received a telephone call from his brother just minutes before the fatal plunge, with Samuel claiming grandly that he was going to swim the length of the river and then join his mother,

Elizabeth Stone (deceased for one year). Lesley reported that he tried to talk his brother out of going near the
river, to no avail. Samuel hung up on him. Locals may
remember that Mrs. Elizabeth Stone died a year ago
today in a fatal one-car crash on the back road to
Catawissa. A side story then gave a short background
of past deaths that had occurred in the Susquehanna
River.

"John Deadly has quite a history with Dr. Stone,
wouldn't you say?" Sheski asked Mike.

"Very true! But that must have been a terrible blow
to Dr. Stone, losing his brother just one year after his
mother's death. I'm surprised he didn't crack. Still, it
seems like our man Stone has a lot of misery attached
to his family. Makes you wonder."

The *Danville News* printed a story on July 29 detailing the eventual discovery of Samuel Stone's body. It
outlined how four Shikellamy High School teenagers
swimming in the river found the young man's body in
shallow water proximate to a small island. The discovery was made at the junction of the north and west
branches of the Susquehanna River, nearby the town of
Northumberland. There were quotes from a concerned
Lesley Stone, who had come home from Harvard to
wait for word on his brother.

Sheski looked but could find no further remarks
from John Deadly. On July 30, an obituary appeared
with an outline of Samuel Stone's short life. He was
born November 24, 1950, at the Bloomsburg Hospital
and graduated from Danville High School in June,

1968. He was a member of the high school football team and played the lead in *Hamlet,* his high school play. Samuel resided at the Stones' family home on West Market Street. A small photo of a handsome young man with shoulder-length blond hair accompanied the article. From the photo, a strong resemblance to his older brother was seen.

Newspaper accounts that Mike found in the paper basically reported the same facts. The only differences were the quotes from unidentified sources. These sources, who preferred to remain anonymous, confirmed reports that, like his brother before him, Samuel had been accepted at Harvard. They further noted that he was unable to attend due to his alternating periods of mania and depression. The sources also said that Samuel had been wildly spending large amounts of cash on all kinds of luxuries for months prior to his death. A much younger attorney Jerry Smithson was also quoted in the article but, unlike the others, preferred not to be anonymous. Conservator of the Stone estate, Smithson stated that he had tried unsuccessfully to curb the carnage on the young man's inheritance. He claimed that this should in no way be a smudge on the reputation of Smithson and Smithson, Attorneys at Law. He informed the readers that the Smithsons were competent attorneys and were open for business six days a week.

"Good grief," Mike said in exasperation. "Smithson even managed a commercial in connection with this tragedy."

"Some things never change," Sheski replied.

He then went on to read the rest of the article. " 'It was rumored that tens of thousands of dollars were charged to his account before the lawyer could put an end to it. When asked, Lesley declined to comment further on his brother's behavior and death.' "

The lieutenants read each article closely, appreciating the way a newspaper gave details and narratives that were quite different than the sometimes sterile police reports. A more rounded picture of the people involved was beginning to emerge. And, if they were to make any headway in the murder at hand, even the smallest thing could make the difference.

There were also occasional personal nuggets about those of interest to the officers, which were gleaned from the social columns that small-town papers are inclined to write. Who had whom over for parties, families vacationing together, and winners in local charity golf tournaments. All of which showed where society locals spent their time, and with whom.

The two went to the copier located under the massive stairway. For fifteen cents a page, they were able to copy the articles relevant to their investigation. When they finished, Mike and Sheski replaced the newspapers on the cart that Marian used. Remembering the librarian's stooped posture and advanced age, Mike pushed the cart up to the desk and asked if he could take it anywhere for her.

Smiling, she thanked them and said no, that she would have a volunteer put them away later. On her desk was a sign remarking on the non-profit status of the library, with small envelopes for donations. Both of the men put money in an envelope and thanked her for her help. On their way out, they handed them to her. She blushed and thanked them profusely, telling them to come visit again. They promised that they would.

After exiting the library building, both state troopers breathed in the fresh air and started walking toward their car. "I think it's time we paid Mr. John Deadly a visit, Mike. What do you think?"

His partner nodded in agreement.

Sheski thought a minute and then said, "Yes, it's definitely time we go see Mr. John Deadly."

Sheski drove a short way and pulled off the main street into a restaurant parking lot. He motioned to the telephone out in front.

"It's your turn to make the call and the car phone's not working," he said to his partner. He handed him Deadly's telephone number.

Mike got out of the car and went over to the pay phone. In the declining light, he looked at the numbers on the slip of paper Sheski gave him. He punched them in. Looking back at his partner, he flipped Sheski a thumbs-up sign. After a few meager sentences, he returned to the car and informed his friend, "Mr. Deadly says he will be there for another hour. If we get there now, we can talk to him."

The detectives followed Deadly's directions.

"Are you sure this is the correct address?" Sheski asked his friend quizzically as he viewed attractive, well-maintained homes lined up neatly in rows. "These all look like the kind of expensive lots that Barry Brown cared for."

"That's the address he gave me five minutes ago," was the reply.

The two were now in one of the more mature and nicer developments to the north of town. They were sitting in front of a meticulously cared-for ranch style home. It nestled in a landscaped yard on a large lot.

The policemen sat and looked at each other. Mike again compared the address Deadly had given him to the one above the door. No doubt about it, they had the right house. Neither officer could believe that the crusty John Deadly lived in such a nice house.

Sheski whistled. "Where could he get the money to buy this?" he rhetorically asked his friend. "I would have thought he lived in a dumpy motel or under a bowling alley or something. Certainly not in a place this nice."

"I'm surprised, too. He lives a lot better on a security man's salary than most. He either owes a bundle or is better off than I would have guessed. By the way, what did the local police tell you about him?"

Sheski began to read aloud the notes that Andy Wallace had given him on Deadly. "John P. Deadly. No middle name, just a P. He's sixty-two years old, born in 1937, graduated from Danville High School in 1955." Sheski droned on. "Had a six-year army career, was a grunt in Vietnam, honorable discharge in 1975. Black belt in karate. Keeps to himself. Man of few words. Never married, no children. Head of security at Stone Haven under Dr. Lesley Stone since the place opened in 1976. Oh yeah, by the way, he served in Vietnam with some other locals we know. Dr. Burns, Gordon Ashman, Bobby Snyder, and here we go again"—he paused for effect—"Dr. Lesley Stone."

Mike raised his eyebrows at the information. Along with everything else, he was not surprised that Deadly had never married.

Chapter Nineteen

The state policeman positioned himself where he had a good view of the alley and the intersection to the rear of Lana's home. He had been stationed there by Lieutenant Sheski, who had telephoned him earlier to see how it was going. He reported the facts. So far, it was quiet.

The unlit home behind him had no activity all evening. Mature landscaping obscured his observance of some of the property but he was certain that this was the best he could do. He sat down and leaned his back against a small tree and lamented having to pull yet another double shift because of staffing problems. The long hours were taking their toll.

The officer had been observing Lana's house for awhile, repositioning himself according to the time of day and his own comfort needs. Nothing much was happening as traffic diminished and he frequently changed his position to keep from dozing off.

He did not see the small figure dressed in black watching him watch the house. When his head bobbed and his chin touched his chest, the figure made its move.

It was getting dark outside now and Lana was starting to feel tired. She peered out the windows at the traffic heading to the bridge. Headlights glared from as far as she could see down Sunbury Road, typical for this time of the day. She then went from window to window in an effort to be reassured that someone wasn't lurking about her property, and scolded herself for feeling so insecure.

After feeding Bunky, she took a hot bath and got into some cozy flannel pajamas and a bathrobe. In his usual manner, the dog followed her all over the house as she tidied up a bit. Lana looked out the windows again and then got a novel from a shelf to read. Bunky was watching her closely in the hopes that she would play with him or that he could grab something she had and hide it from her.

Placing her tired feet into sheepskin slippers, Lana went into the television room, sank deep into her favorite overstuffed chair, and reviewed the day's events. She had gone back to work at 8 A.M. that morning and was busy all day.

All of the Stone Haven staff was abuzz about the murders, trying to figure out whodunnit. Most agreed that just about anyone could have done Rose in. No one liked her, they reasoned. Lana was the only one who ever had anything nice to say about her, they would note sarcastically. Of course, they would complain, Lana hardly ever said anything bad about anyone. Staff members tried to have their discussions discreetly because of the potential effect should any patients or even Dr. Stone overhear them. A couple of times, Lana had walked in on their gatherings, heads together, talking. They would turn toward her, look a little sheepish, and then continue in low voices. She was sure that a couple of times the talk was about her and Sheski. She hadn't told them anything and it was driving them crazy. Especially when she had a visit with him in her office for a few minutes.

Lana reminisced about how working with a small staff such as this was much better than the hordes of personnel she was accustomed to at larger general hospitals. Her past experiences with gossips in those places were a lot worse. Everyone was a target, sooner or later, for vicious rumors. She didn't want to think about it.

Lana was deep in thought when she heard Bunky growling. The low growls increased to whines and yips, his little butt moving back and forth as he pranced about the house. He finally ended up in the kitchen sniffing the crease at the bottom of the door and looking up expectantly at the door window.

Reluctantly, Lana got out of her chair and went to the kitchen in the back of the house to see what all the fuss was about. She flipped the light switch on, illuminating an area directly outside the back door. Darkness obscured her view of the rest of the yard. Bunky continued his noise-making.

"What's the matter, boy?" she asked nervously. "Do you hear something? Has that skunk come back again?"

Cautiously, Lana unlocked the door, then the storm door, and proceeded to step outside. Thinking back later, she would regret not having called the police instead. She would also regret not remaining inside locked doors.

Her flannel bathrobe securely wrapped around her slender body, and expecting to see a black furry creature with a white stripe down its back, Lana gingerly made her way down the two steps onto the small brick patio. The last thing she remembered was the feel of the bricks beneath her slippers and then . . . nothing.

When she finally came to, she was shivering and lying on her side on a cold, hard surface. The back of her head was pounding with pain. She reached for the area of discomfort and felt a warm, sticky substance at the base of her skull, oozing down her neck, slowly dripping across the front of her pajamas. She leaned on her right hand and tried to focus her eyes, but had trouble adjusting to the dark. Finally, she could make out the outline of the hard brick beneath her. *I'm on the patio,* she thought. *What am I doing here? What happened?*

After a few moments, she remembered. Her dog had been barking and she had stepped outside to see what he was growling at. She reasoned that someone must have come up from behind her and struck her on the head. Her thoughts raced. *Where's Bunky? Did he come out when I did?* Fear gripped her. *How long have I been lying here? Is the attacker still here?* She struggled to her feet, grabbing an iron railing for support. Looking about through misty eyes, all seemed eerily quiet.

The dull pain in the back of her skull was debilitating, and she was starting to get sick. Feeling nauseated, Lana began to worry about shock setting in. The loss of blood, the cold weather, all could throw her into a state of shock. She shakily grabbed the hem of her flannel robe and pressed it against the back of her head. That's when she started retching. When she was finished, Lana wiped her mouth on her sleeve. She had to find her pet.

"Bunky! Bunky! Where are you?" She was screaming as loud as her aching head would permit. She knew that the small dog could not defend himself, and that brought her close to hysterics. *I've got to remain calm,* she kept telling herself. *Maybe he's inside the house.*

Lana knew her three-year-old pet well. She had raised him from a one-and-a-half-pound puppy, nurturing him through ear infections and kennel cough. He would not bark in reply. He never did. Whenever he got himself in a predicament, he just sat and waited for her to find him. Which, in the past, she'd managed to do.

She entered the wide open back door, and searching the downstairs, realized what had taken place here. Someone had torn apart her house! She knew that if Bunky got outside, she would never find him. Drawers were pulled out, the contents spilled onto the floors. Cushions were off the furniture, and her desk and filing cabinets had been ransacked! Pictures were yanked off the walls and thrown about. What could they have been looking for? The sick feeling in her gut was beginning to return. *I've got to find him,* she was telling herself.

"Bunky, are you here?" she called repeatedly. "Where are you?" By now, tears covered her face in anticipation of finding his tiny lifeless body. *If anyone hurt my dog,* she thought, *he won't have a place to hide!*

Lana picked up a Mickey Mantle autographed baseball bat from the floor of her computer room and pushed her back against the wall. Her head was still hurting and she felt warm blood on the back of her neck. She again pressed the hem of her robe to the wound and winced in pain. Stooping down, she grabbed her telephone from the floor, where it must have fallen when the intruder was going through her desk. Dialing 911, she waited for the voice at the other end. In response to efficient questioning, Lana whispered her situation into the receiver, gave her name, address, and directions to her house, worriedly scanning the room in fear of the intruder hearing her. After she gave them the information, the dispatcher asked her to remain on the line but she said no, that she wanted to find her dog. She hung up and went around the corner to the back stairwell. She pressed the light switch, peered into the front rooms first, and then proceeded slowly up the back staircase.

The crystal light at the top of the stair illuminated the steps and the upstairs hall. Her back against the stair wall, baseball bat in hand, she slowly took each step, ears pricked for any sound. There was none. At the upstairs landing, a quick decision was made to check her bathroom first. Lana switched the baseball bat into her left hand and pressed her right hand against her bathroom door. It slowly opened. Light from the hallway streamed in, illuminating the corners of the room. She was thankful not to see anyone there. *But where is Bunky? And why aren't the police here by now?*

Lana replaced the bat into her right hand and proceeded through the bathroom, then into a short hallway that led to her bedroom. Her left hand found the switch on the wall and she turned it on. Personal belongings were scattered about the room. Whoever had gone through the downstairs had been up here, too.

She began to get scared again. The earlier fear that had given way to desperation in trying to find her dog was now returning. What if the intruder was hiding here? She slowly bent down and looked under the bed, praying to God that she wouldn't find someone there. Relieved, she then straightened and eyed the closet door. Taking a deep breath, she put her hand on the closet door handle and opened it wide. Heart pounding hard against her chest, she pulled the bare light bulb string. She could see the clothes that had been pulled off the rack and lay in a heap on the floor. Whatever her attacker was looking for, he obviously hadn't found yet.

It was then that her heart leaped for joy. In the corner, sitting quietly on her discarded wardrobe, was Bunky! "There you are," she screamed. "Thank God, you're all right. I was so worried." She picked her small dog up into her arms and kissed the top of his head. He, in turn, licked her face. *He must have gotten in here at some point during the intrusion, and the closet door was closed behind him,* she thought.

Now that Lana had found Bunky, she became more rational and realized that she needed to get to safety. Her knees became weak and the room started to spin. She crumpled to the floor in a dead faint. She never heard the distant police siren coming her way.

Chapter Twenty

Sheski and Mike waited patiently on the front porch for John Deadly to answer the doorbell. They rang it again. Despite the inevitable cold reception that lay ahead, they were anticipating this appointment. Visiting suspects in their own home always provided the lieutenants with so much insight into the target's inner life and personality. Many things that were kept hidden in the outside world were often revealed in some way in their own home. A place they considered safe. A place that reflected their personal taste and lifestyle.

After a short time, the door was opened. Deadly was dressed in blue jeans and a flannel shirt, with his tam perched to one side of his head. He gruffly invited the investigators into his living room. They passed through a short hallway lined with artwork and then into the modern great room. Their host gestured for them to take seats anywhere.

Looking about, Sheski chose the brown leather couch and Mike seated himself next to him. Deadly lowered himself into a matching wing-backed, brown leather chair. A large hand-made blue and gray pottery lamp with the words *Danville, PA* glazed on the front was perched in the middle of an accompanying stand. Sheski spoke first.

"We're here to ask you some questions in reference to the Rose Stone murder case. These are just preliminary questions, you understand. At some point, we will want to talk to you in our office."

"Sure. I told you I would help you all I can," Deadly replied sullenly.

"Where were you at the time of the murder of Rose Stone?" Mike began.

He did not hesitate. "I was with Dr. Stone at the hospital. It was a professional call. We were together for a couple of hours. I don't have to tell you about it, you know, client-doctor privilege and all," he said petulantly.

"Okay for now, but at some point you may want to say more," Mike said.

"Are you aware that the body of Barry Brown has been discovered?" Sheski asked abruptly.

"Yes, I am," he replied. "Heard it on my scanner. Probably killed himself after killing Rose, don't you think?" He reached over absently to straighten the lamp.

"No, we don't think so. The coroner believes that Barry Brown was murdered about the same time as Rose," Sheski replied. "We may be looking for a killer who murdered Rose and then, for some reason, killed Barry Brown, too."

He watched Deadly's face closely for any response. There was none. A vein below the tam perched over his right ear pulsed rapidly. Other than that, there was nothing to read. His eyes remained focused on his inquisitors, his hands were steady, and his breathing regular.

He's a cool one, thought Sheski. *And I've seen a lot of guilty cool ones.* He knew that the guilty ones didn't always give themselves away with their expressions or body language. Experience and training had taught him that sociopaths were quite capable of remaining calm and composed through the toughest interrogations. They could look you right in the eye and lie at the same time. No remorse, no regret, no conscience. They took no responsibility for their actions. It was always someone else's fault, not theirs. Therefore, many believed that they didn't need therapy. After all, there was nothing wrong with them. So watching Deadly nonchalantly handle their questions was no surprise.

"We have reason to believe that Rose's killer was still there at the property when the body was discovered. You see, when Miss Stahl was checking out the garden, she witnessed someone in the back of the property with a garden tool. At first, we thought it was Barry Brown. Now, I don't think so. I think it was the killer. I think whoever murdered Rose was interrupted by the gardener and killed him, too. Then he was interrupted, again, by Miss Stahl. The killer saw her coming into the garden before she saw him. He didn't have time to run to where his vehicle was parked and get away. Besides, that would have looked very suspicious. So he took a chance and just stood there with the murder weapon, the gardening tool, as if he was working."

"Sounds to me like there's a lot of guessing going on here," Deadly said with a smirk.

"Maybe," Sheski replied, smirking also. "If I'm right, that means our killer is probably very close to the same size as Barry Brown, five-foot-six, or close to that. How tall are you, Mr. Deadly?"

Mike was looking at his partner in surprise. He hadn't expected him to reveal so much of their case. *Sheski must be on to something,* he thought.

Deadly smiled. It was a hard smile accompanied by hard eyes. "About that. But there must be hundreds of people in this town that height or close to it, men and women alike. That's no big deal. Besides, I heard you found Rose's missing jewelry on Barry's body. Maybe he killed her and then committed suicide."

"That may be the killer's biggest mistake," Mike said slowly. "They always make some kind of a mistake, you know. It can be as simple as a bad choice for their partner in crime, or something more complicated. There's no such thing as the perfect crime. We don't have all the details of Barry's murder, yet. But, before we're finished, we will." He wanted to sound confident and did.

The security man appeared to be unimpressed.

"People don't kill themselves by wrapping wire about their own neck, Deadly. Especially Barry Brown. He didn't have the physical strength or dexterity it would have taken. As good a gardener as he was, it was remarkable that he was able to do such perfect work with his impairment. You see, the medicine he was taking was starting to cause some side effects. Barry Brown was suffering from drug-induced Parkinsonism. He was getting no relief from other drugs he was taking to relieve those symptoms. According to his physician, Barry was experiencing muscle rigidity, tremors, and a shuffling gait. That's why he had that expressionless look that everyone thought was due to his psychosis. He didn't change his expression because he couldn't. He was an easy target for his killer. Barry Brown didn't have the capability of defending himself. Poor guy was in the wrong place at the wrong time."

Deadly looked bored.

"Oh, by the way, the Darling Diamond was not found with the body. Dr. Stone was real unhappy when he got that news." Sheski waited a minute for his words to sink in. Mike sat motionless next to him, observing their host.

"Well, as I told you, all this has nothing to do with me," Deadly said. "I was with Dr. Stone at the time of these murders. You're accusing the wrong guy."

"I'm not accusing you of anything," Sheski said. "We're just here to ask a few questions. I did some reading at the library today, and there's something I was wondering about."

Deadly started to perk up. His body stiffened and he gazed intently at the lieutenant, waiting for the other shoe to drop.

"I read that you were the only eye witness when Samuel Stone went into the river. What happened there?"

Deadly got hold of himself and loosened his grip on the chair arms. "I have nothing to add to what you read. That was a long time ago and I'm not sure if I remember the details. The poor kid was crazy. There was no stopping him. What are you snooping around into that old story for?" he demanded.

"Just filling in some blanks," Mike said.

Sheski looked Deadly full in the face and stated, "Those old newspapers held some interesting stories."

Before Deadly could inquire further, Sheski reached for the pager that was buzzing against his right hip. *Good timing,* he thought. *Let him wonder what else we know.* He reached down to turn the pager so he could read the message, and saw Andy Wallace's office number gliding in view.

"We gotta go, but we'll be in touch," he said to his host.

The three men got out of their seats and headed toward the front door, the lieutenants leading the way. On the way out, something caught Sheski's eye. Among the pictures in the hallway was a gold-framed three-by-four oil painting of an elderly man that looked decades old. It was a picture of a pleasant, though unsmiling, face that conveyed an air of mystery. A full head of white hair was pulled away from his face and tied in the back with a string. He was wearing a white high-necked shirt buttoned up the front. Something about that picture was puzzling to Sheski. He furrowed his brows and looked closer. *What is it?*

"Don't you have to be going?" snorted Deadly, placing himself between the trooper and the picture under scrutiny.

As Sheski turned to go, he saw on the frame a brass plaque with the caption SELF-PORTRAIT painted in black. In the lower left corner rested a *P* with a fragile-looking urchin in the loop. Sheski looked at Mike, glanced back at the signature, then back to his partner. Their eyes locked for a split-second. *My God,* Sheski thought, realizing what was puzzling him. *I almost missed it. A key piece of this case was right before my eyes, and I almost missed it.*

In the car, Sheski revealed his suspicions to Mike. He then placed a call to Andy. Before he could ask the town cop what he wanted, he heard the news about Lana. He was reassured that she was alive and okay, just pretty upset about the intruder. Her head wound was minor, although like most scalp wounds, it bled freely.

The lieutenants rushed to Lana's home in Riverside. When they arrived, police cars with flashing lights were parked out in front, impeding traffic. There were already several investigators milling around, examining the crime scene.

Sheski spotted Doug, the new young trooper, on the front sidewalk with a flashlight, looking around in the darkness. He got out of the car and yelled, "Where the hell was my man? Someone was supposed to be guarding her around the clock!"

Red-faced, Doug informed Sheski that Trooper Moore was posted at the Stahl home. He was found by the local police, out cold next to the alley, when they came to investigate Lana's 911 call. "Whoever struck Lana was probably the one who got her guardian, too.

Moore is recuperating at home with a nasty headache and a bruised ego," Doug explained.

"Where's Lana?" Mike asked one of the officers.

"She's in the living room on the couch," was the reply. "Refuses to go to the hospital. Her physician came here and examined her. You just missed him. He said she's gonna be okay. She just needs some rest."

Mike nodded to Sheski to go on in. His friend motioned for him to go with him and they quietly entered the living room. When they approached the couch, Lana's eyes were closed. Her face was pale and drawn. She was on her side with her legs drawn up to her chest, a granny-stitch afghan thrown over her. Bunky was lying next to her. He stirred and looked up when Sheski and Mike drew near.

"Hi, Tommy," she said with a weak voice. Then she frowned. "I was stupid. I shouldn't have gone out there."

"Hey, it's okay," he said quietly, looking at the mess about him. "Are you all right? That's the important thing."

"I still have a terrible headache, but I'll be fine. I just need to rest. What were they after? What could I possibly have that they want?"

That was one thing Sheski didn't know, but was determined to find out. He had a hunch, but needed to see some more people first.

"I don't know," he answered truthfully. "Now, you get some rest and I'll find some help to clean this up when the police are through here."

"Thanks, Tommy."

His own name was the last thing he heard from her lips as she drifted off to a much-needed sleep. He kissed her damp forehead and went out to hear the details from Andy.

"I want two men guarding her place, round the clock," Sheski said to a trooper. "One inside, one outside. If she complains, tell her to talk to me." The trooper nodded.

Chapter Twenty-one

Bobby Snyder had company, and they were busy with paperwork at his office on Mill Street when Sheski and Mike arrived. As usual, Bobby was engrossed in business, hard at work on some bids for more property that had recently come up for sale. It had been a buyer's market for a while and he was taking advantage of it.

When they entered, Bobby recognized them as cops and bid a hasty good-bye to his real estate agent, promising to call him later. The agent gave Bobby a questioning look as he went out the front door. Bobby shrugged his shoulders in return.

The lieutenants flashed their badges and told Bobby that they wanted a few minutes of his time.

He extended his hand and encouraged them to take a seat. *What the hell do they want?* he wondered.

Sheski wasted no time in asking him where he was at the time of Rose's murder. They were already informed

185

of the downtown development deal and how the restoration of the storefronts would have devastated him financially if Rose had lived to have her way. *Unless he has some pretty good answers,* Sheski thought, *Bobby's not off the long list of suspects.*

"I was here at my office, going over some accounts. The Restoration Committee meeting was that night and I wanted to be prepared for Rose's barrage. She was always trying to throw her weight around to accomplish what she thought this town needed. Hey, I have nothing to hide," he said, flinging a pencil that he had been holding onto his desk.

"I was so sick of her finding ways of spending someone else's money. I worked damn hard for mine. Nobody handed me anything for free. Rose had hers given to her. Never did any real work in her whole life. She kept promising that if we agreed to restore the main street, building fronts, sidewalks, light fixtures, stuff like that, she would help us gain some funding. You know, grants and donations, that kind of thing." He ran thin fingers through his light brown hair.

"Many of the committee members disagreed with Rose," Bobby went on. "But they were afraid to go against her. She had a lot of power in this town. Rose had money in her own right and wasn't afraid to use it. Her husband had his own bucks, too. This is a small town. People here are highly influenced by that. She could just about get her way on anything she wanted. It would have ruined me. I own more than half of this side of Mill Street. No way could I afford to comply with what she wanted to push through. It would have wiped me out."

"So, with Rose out of the way, I guess you won't have to worry about that now, will you?" Sheski suggested.

"I know there are people who are gossiping and pointing the finger at me. Well, I didn't do it," he retorted. "I may be coarse and from the other side of the tracks, but I'm no killer. Besides, what about Barry Brown? That lunatic could have done it. He was goofy enough."

"Then you haven't heard? Barry turned up in Mahoning Creek yesterday afternoon . . . dead. And it wasn't suicide. The coroner thinks he was murdered about the same time as Rose Stone. He's off our list of suspects."

Bobby's eyebrows went up and an "Ohhhhhhh" escaped from surprised lips.

"Is there anyone who can vouch for your whereabouts at the time of both murders?" Sheski asked.

"My secretary was with me that day until two P.M. She'll tell you. Then she had to leave to pick her son up from the babysitter. I stayed around just like I said until it was time to go to the meeting. No one there knew anything about Rose's murder. And I heard about it the next day on the news. We just figured something came up so she couldn't make it. I have to admit, most of us were glad when she didn't show."

Bobby told all this in a whiny, complaining voice. The voice of one who was familiar with getting blamed for things he didn't do.

"How long have you known Dr. Stone, Bobby?"

Sheski inquired. He thought there might be a story in that shared Vietnam experience that the town police had mentioned. It was a hunch that unleashed a flood of venom.

"That bastard," Bobby said angrily. "I've known him since a bunch of us from town got sent to 'Nam."

He fumbled with some documents on his desk and then faced his inquisitors squarely.

"I served in the Army with John Deadly, Lesley Stone, Gordon Ashman, and Richard Burns. What a crew. At first there was a lot of camaraderie, you know, being from town and all. We were at a base camp north of Saigon and missed our hometown, our families, and our girlfriends. Our division was serving as a buffer between Saigon and the enemy's base areas in Tay Ninh Province. We were all in the same hell, rich and poor alike.

"After we got settled in, though, it began to change," he went on. "Things began to get a little tense. Every Friday night was poker night. There were games all over the area. Ours was always the best, though," he bragged. "We had the best players. Players with plenty of money, and the biggest pots. Out of our bunch, Ashman was the only one who didn't join in. Didn't believe in gambling, he told us. I respected him for that," he said in a softer tone. "Ashman was a good man with high standards, and he always treated me all right." Bobby paced the floor a little, looking out the front window once or twice, and then went on.

"Many a grunt made big money in 'Nam playing cards. Most of them sent it home to their families. I personally made over twenty grand at the poker table the first year alone. I wired it home to Julie, my wife, and told her to start buying property with it. She began to buy up Mill Street. She put the winnings down on buildings and then made monthly payments by renting them out and using her own earnings as a teacher. Properties were a lot cheaper then. Anyway, I may have been poor, but I was good at poker. Stone was not." He laughed a little at that. "And he was tight, too," Bobby went on. "He hated losing. I've met a lot of people from all walks of life, and I never met anyone that hated to lose money like Stone. He bet big and lost big. And he begrudged every dime."

Sheski and Mike were entranced. Bobby was spilling his guts and the lieutenants were convinced he was telling the truth.

Bobby got out of his chair, bristling at the memories. He walked around his desk, gesturing as he spoke.

"It was bad enough we had to watch our backs because of the enemy. The Viet Cong had tunnels under us that made our lives even more miserable than they already were. We never did clean them out of there. It then got so we had to watch some of our friends, too. Stone and Deadly started to get real tight. Deadly became his flunkey. He did anything that Stone wanted. They spent a lot of time with their heads together, hatching schemes."

At this point Bobby looked puzzled. "For some reason, the MPs were watching Deadly day and night. I don't know what that was all about, but everyone knew something big was going on. A couple of times, he got beat up by some of the locals. They usually didn't both-er us, but they sure hated Deadly. He musta ticked them off real bad. One time, four of them ganged up on him at the edge of the camp and damn near killed him. It took that many to get the best of him. He's a tough one. If the MPs hadn't stepped in, he woulda been listed MIA."

"What about Lesley Stone?" Mike asked.

"Stone always had money," Bobby replied. "And it was the most important thing to him. You know, his family had plenty, so it's not like he needed more. But he wanted it. To Stone, money was right up there above duty, honor, and country. He and Deadly had all kinds of sidelines to bring in cash. Most of it was typ-ical GI stuff—-booze, loans, cigarettes, supplies. And some of that loot went to pay gambling losses. You'd think a guy that worshipped money like he did would avoid a pastime that he regularly lost at. Not Stone. I think he believed he'd eventually win it all back. Once in awhile he did win a little, but most of the time he didn't. Everyone was better at poker than he was." He snickered.

Bobby again paced to the window and then turned back to his guests.

"Stone's anger over his losses came to a head the last month I was stationed there. It was Friday night and we were playing our usual game in the recreation tent. This game was really big, our biggest. On the final hand, the pot held more than five grand. The last three holding cards were Burns, Stone, and me. Burns folded. That left Stone and me. The tent was full, and the word got out that there was a huge pot at stake. Guys were crowding in, standing room only, to see how it would all come out. It was hot and smoky in there, and we were all drinking and starting to get tired. Stone and I were taking our time, though. He wanted that pot so bad his eyes were glazed over with greed. I wanted it, too. You see, the wife had written to tell me about a four-story building, a former hotel, that had just gone on the market here. I wanted that building. It would have fit in quite nicely with the rest of our properties. Winning the hand would have meant that she could go ahead and buy it."

"Stone and I were studying each other closely. He was cool as could be. You see, he was holding good cards, real good cards. I figured he must have gotten lucky and had something or he would have folded earlier. You could never be sure with him, though. How a guy so book-smart could be so crummy at poker is beyond me. As for me, I was sweating buckets. I had good cards, too. But I knew that with the hand I had, something was bound to happen. The sweat was rolling down my face and the moment so powerful that I never made a move to stop it. For the first time in my poker career, I was carrying a Dead Man's Hand."

"Aces and eights," Mike said knowingly.

"Yep. I'm not usually a superstitious man, but when it comes to cards, I don't tempt fate. I finally called him, and the cards went down. For as big as the crowd was, you could have heard a pin drop that night. Stone had three tens and some face cards. My heart was in my throat as I slowly lay down the three aces and two black eights. Guys started muttering things like "Holy shit" and "Look out" when those cards hit the wood. You see, they knew the cards . . . and they knew Stone. They figured he wasn't going to take the loss well. He had a lot of money on that table and I just took it away from him. The look on his face was one I will never forget. It was evil, pure evil. Stone never said a word. He looked at Deadly and then he looked back at me. I didn't like what I was seeing. The other guys backed away, leaving a path for him to get through as he sullenly made his way out the door. Before he left, he looked back at me again, one last time, that foul look on his face."

"I was tired and staggered back to my tent. I counted my winnings and came up with more than five-thousand-two-hundred dollars. That was a lot of money back then, and the biggest haul I ever made at poker. And I've played a lot of cards. Naturally, I was overjoyed about the win, but I was concerned about where to keep all that until I could send it home. I couldn't believe my good fortune. I was gonna own the lynchpin in my row of properties on Mill Street. Life was good. I was really tired and could barely keep my eyes open, so I found what I thought was the best place to put it. Ever since I joined the Army, I carried with me, for luck, an old calfskin Civil War haversack. Gordon Ashman gave it to me for good luck when he heard we were gonna serve together in 'Nam. He said it was used for holding ammo by a Yankee who survived Gettysburg. Anyway, I decided to put my winnings in my lucky haversack and put that under my pillow for safekeeping. The night was hot, humid, and quiet. Charlie was staying underground and we were dug in for the long haul. I don't remember falling asleep, it happened so quickly. Slept in my uniform, I guess. I don't recall anything else until the next morning when I woke up in the hospital tent with a banger of a headache. Seems that when I didn't show for breakfast, a couple of my buddies went looking for me. What they found was my ransacked tent. My belongings were strewn all over the place, and I was out cold. When they couldn't rouse me, they called the medics and I was taken for some emergency treatment. The docs figured I had a drunk on and were angry and saying I was wasting their time. I kept telling them I didn't have that much to drink. I never drink much when I'm playing cards. It ruins my game."

He paused a minute and then said, "I think someone slipped something into my drink right before I went back to my tent. Eventually, I came around but had nothing but the headache to show for my night. I searched under my pillow and my haversack with my winnings was gone! I can't prove it, but I know Stone and his stooge Deadly had something to do with it. The MPs wouldn't do anything. Said I couldn't even prove I had that kind of money on me at the time. The few witnesses they spoke to claimed I was drunk and could barely walk when they saw me heading back to my tent. The day after the game, Stone and Deadly acted as if nothing happened. But they were a hell of a lot happier than they had been the night before."

Bobby sat on his desk and thoughtfully fingered an autographed baseball resting on a plastic stand. "Greatest hitter to ever live," he said, looking at the inscription. "He never gave up. Practiced all the time. That's what made him so great. He was a veteran, too." He looked at Ted Williams' signature and placed the ball back on its perch. Bobby then looked up at the two policemen.

"I've never forgotten what those two did over there. Remembered it all whenever I had any dealings with them back home here. Stone went on to med school, married a wealthy young lady, and opened Stone Haven. Deadly went to work for him from day one. It's been a successful venture for Stone. There's a lot of money in providing psychiatric care for rich crazy people. Not that he needed it," he said as an aside.

"By then," Bobby went on, "Stone was sole heir to the family fortune. But again, he never had enough. If his brother had lived much longer, though, there may not have been much left, the way that maniac was spending it. That would have served Stone right after what he did to me."

Bobby had been slowly pacing about his office, reliving past events for the policemen. When he finished, he looked drained.

Sheski and Mike had listened without interruption. It provided some insight into what they were dealing with at Stone Haven, but Bobby wouldn't be off the list of suspects until he provided an alibi. After all, maybe he sought to get back at Stone by killing his wife and stealing her jewelry. That would pay him back for what he lost in 'Nam, with some left over. The diamond she was wearing was worth a lot and hasn't been found yet. Maybe Bobby had stashed it away for a future opportunity. By murdering Rose, he would kill two birds with one stone, no pun intended. She would be off his back about the downtown restoration and Lesley Stone would have gotten what he had coming to him. *You're not off the hook yet, Bobby,* thought Sheski.

"We've got another appointment soon," Mike reminded his partner.

"Right. Thanks, Bobby, for your candor and your time," Sheski offered sincerely. "If you think of anything else that may be of help to us, or if there's anything else you want to tell us, give us a call."

The two investigators stood on the granite front stoop of Bobby Snyder's office, watching traffic on downtown Mill Street. It was at a stop now, because a train was thundering through the main thoroughfare, bisecting the town at forty miles per hour. They were glad for the interruption; they had wanted a few minutes to digest everything they had just heard.

"He has more than one motive," said Mike, looking over at his partner.

"But he didn't have to tell us the 'Nam story," Sheski countered. "He wanted to make the point of what a money-grubber that Stone is. So much so that Stone didn't mind doing a fellow soldier out of more than five grand."

He watched the last boxcar fly past just ten feet from idling vehicles.

"And what's the connection between Stone and Deadly?"

"Birds of a feather." Mike said. "From what I see, both of them have sociopathic personalities. And those kind often seek out others just like themselves to associate with."

"Maybe. But there has to be more to it than that. These two come from the opposite sides of the track. Dr. Stone is polished and articulate. Deadly is crude and callous. They seemingly have nothing in common. I wonder what happened in 'Nam to make those two really tight."

"They have some kind of a bond," Mike said. "And Deadly lives pretty good, for a security officer. I can't get that out of my mind. That Pratt self-portrait must be worth a fortune. How could he afford to own an original Pratt? Especially the most sought-after one. Hey . . ." Mike said, looking at his watch. "We'd better get going. Didn't we say we'd meet Jess Walter at Karen Stone's at eleven? It's quarter of, now."

"I'll drive this time," Sheski said to his partner.

Chapter Twenty-two

With Sheski behind the wheel, they headed toward the river. Jess had finally gotten in touch with them after they had repeatedly tried to contact him. He had called Sheski at his office first thing that morning to tell him that he wanted to meet with them. They agreed with Jess to gather at Karen's farm, but made it clear that they would be talking on the record.

Coming off the bridge, the first house they passed was Lana's. Sheski tapped the car horn twice to let her know he was going by. He had promised to signal her on the way. He was relieved to know, after talking to her earlier, that she was feeling better, although, understandably, still achy. Their car cruised past the quaint Riverside homes. Old Victorians, cottages, and other early structures of all styles and sizes lined Sunbury Road.

The men made small talk about the case, all the while enjoying the scenery. *I could live here,* Sheski thought.

At the Methodist Church, they turned left, gradually leaving the charming village and entering the countryside. Farm homes ensconced by shade maples became distanced from one another, separated by silent, swaying fields of wheat, soybeans, and occasional Holstein herds in pastures. Barns with silos, old chicken coops, and corn cribs accompanied their main structures.

Soon, they were again on Karen Stone's lane and Sheski parked the vehicle facing the exit. They weren't expecting any trouble here, but you never knew. He pointed out Jess Walter's vehicle to Mike. It was parked behind the house.

"Probably so no one would know he spent the night here," Mike suggested. "As if you could keep anything from neighbors in any community."

Farmers were no different from anyone else. They kept an eye out for what was going on. In fact, they were usually better historians than most people, working outside and around their properties all day.

Karen and Jess met them at the door, immediately inquiring if there was anything new about her mother's killer. The two policemen assured them that they were busy on the case and that nothing solid had developed. Karen seemed relaxed. She was dressed in an expensively tailored English riding habit and explained that she had been out exercising her Tennessee Walker. She looked good in jodhpurs and knew it, Jess offered them freshly-brewed coffee while Karen excused herself to slip into something else.

The men made small talk and enjoyed the coffee while waiting for their hostess. Surprisingly, she was gone just a few minutes, and returned wearing blue jeans and a white vee-neck T-shirt and moccasins. She looked comfortable. Jess was wearing his usual khaki chinos and a long-sleeved flannel shirt. He, too, had moccasins on. They looked good together.

Sheski cast a glance at Karen's pinky finger where the miniature Darling Diamond had rested.

"It was lovely, wasn't it," she said softly, catching his look. "But I'm not sorry for what I did. I really feel better, as if a load has been lifted." She rubbed her hands together as if to dispel the cold.

"I don't think I ever saw anything quite so beautiful," Sheski replied.

"That's because you haven't seen the ring it was modeled after," she countered. "Mother positively adored that ring. She would never have parted with it. Wore it everywhere. It's not like she did any real work or anything, so it was always cared for."

"How much do you think it was worth?" Mike asked.

"I haven't any idea of its value but it would bring quite a sum. The thief will have a hard time unloading it, though, because the Darling Diamond is such a well-known stone. It came into Father's possession with such provenance. Do you know the story behind it?"

Both men shook their heads.

"It was owned by my grandmother, Elizabeth

Hastings Stone. She loved spending her money and buying things. Gramma Stone was familiar with all of the big city auctions and obtained the Darling Diamond at a private sale that Christie's held. When some personal effects of the actor Clark Gable were auctioned off by his pregnant widow, Gramma placed her successful bid by telephone." Karen laughed and said, "Father told me that Grampa Stone left her do whatever she wanted with her money. He adored her. Father always faulted Grampa for that. Thought that Grampa should have had charge of all the family income."

"Anyway," Karen went on. "Mr. Gable allegedly received the perfect square diamond from the Duke of Windsor during one of his visits to Great Britain. It was labeled the Darling Diamond because The Duke told everyone who ever saw it, in his delightful British accent, that it was 'just darling.' Rumor has it that the Duchess wanted him to keep it for her, but it was one of the few times she didn't get her way. So, you see, it has quite a history behind it. Right before I was born, Father commissioned his New York jeweler to find a similar smaller one for me. He gave it to me on my tenth birthday."

"That's quite a story," said Sheski.

"There's more," Karen continued. "Father almost didn't get the Darling Diamond. Gramma Stone was planning a charitable foundation before her death. She was going to sell it and donate the proceeds, along with most of her estate to the foundation. After her death, Father decided not to go through with it and kept everything, including the diamond, for himself. Even though

Mother wore it, Father never considered that diamond to be hers, you know. It was like he was just lending it to her to wear. He always told her that he wanted it back. She'd just laugh at him."

At this point Karen's voice started to crack and a tear trickled down her cheek. Her hands were trembling and she leaned on her fiancé for support. Jess lovingly put his arm around her and pulled her close.

After a couple of minutes, she composed herself and said, "Jess called you here today because he wanted to talk to you about his whereabouts the day Mother was murdered." She looked up at her lover.

"First of all," Jess began, "Let me set something straight. I did not murder Karen's mother. She and I didn't have a good relationship because of my engagement to Karen, but I didn't want to harm her. Actually, I felt sorry for her. She had few, if any, real friends. You must know, by now, that she wielded her money and power like a laser, cutting down anyone who got in the way of her wants. I'm sure Karen won't mind my saying that's why Rose and her daughter couldn't get along."

Karen nodded her head in agreement.

"It's true that they gave in to Karen's demands for material things all her life," Jess said, "But she harangued Karen on everything from her friends to her choice of colleges. Karen wanted to go to Bucknell to be closer to home and her mother insisted she go to her own alma mater, Stanford. When Karen gave in and went to Stanford, her mother wanted her to major in business like she did, even though Karen's real interest was art. So, to keep peace, Karen majored in business at Stanford. No matter what she did, it was never enough. Rose had to control everything. After her graduation from Stanford, Karen opened her studio. Later, she took graduate courses in art at Bucknell. We share a love for watercolors and met to discuss her work. A relationship blossomed, and the rest is history. When we first met, Karen was guarded and insecure. As our love matured, so did Karen. She gained self-esteem and has changed a lot," he said, looking lovingly at her. "She's talented and makes a good living from her work. That gave her the independence she needed. Rose's threats of writing her out of her will held little interest for Karen. She knows she can make it on her own."

"What about the day of Rose's murder, Jess? Where were you?" Sheski asked.

"For most of the morning I was at my office grading papers. I was distracted, though, by Karen's estrangement from her parents and couldn't keep my mind on my work. After thinking about it for a while, I decided to leave the campus and go to Sweetriver. I arrived there about two P.M. I thought that if I talked to Rose, maybe I could make her understand my love for her daughter and how important it would be for them to reconcile, for everyone's sake. That's why Karen couldn't get me when she called my office. I wasn't there."

"Did you see anyone else around the property when you were there?" Mike asked.

"Barry Brown was in front of the house, trimming shrubbery. He looked up when I arrived but didn't wave or anything, just nodded his head slowly. I waved in return."

"Are you sure it was Barry, and not someone else?" Sheski inquired.

"I'm sure. I recognized him from his picture in the paper after his murder. It was Barry, all right."

"What happened next?"

"I rang the front doorbell and after about a minute, Rose answered it. She had the nerve to tell me to go around to the side door. I guess I wasn't good enough to come through the main entrance. I swallowed my pride and did it. We were in the kitchen, sitting down. She asked what I wanted. Said she wasn't going to give me anything so not to ask. I told her I didn't want anything, that I was there to implore her to reach out to Karen. I told her how important family was to me and that, for Karen's sake, I wanted to put the past behind us and make a new start." He frowned as he recalled Rose's reaction.

"She started to laugh at me. Said she wasn't interested in a relationship with her daughter unless I was out of her life. She even told me that she had hired a private detective to find out everything he could about me. She admitted to being real disappointed to find out I came from a respectable background."

Jess drank some of his coffee and then continued. "Both of my parents were tenured professors at Rutgers University, and financially stable. I reassured her that I didn't want her money. I said I'd be willing to sign a prenuptial agreement, that I loved Karen and only wanted her, not her money. Rose laughed again. Said I was lying, that all men were interested in a woman's money. She said she knew that her husband married her only for her money, too. But she had a surprise coming for him. Rose admitted to planning on rewriting her will. She said that if her husband couldn't be faithful to her, and her daughter was going to marry someone like me, then she would take them both out of her will."

He shook his head back and forth as if unable to comprehend such reasoning, Karen looked pained at the recounting of her mother's behavior.

"Rose said her will would include the donation of all her money and possessions to the restoration of downtown Danville," Jess went on. "As long as they followed her strict instructions for spending it, it was theirs. Good old Rose. She would try to get her own way after her death, too."

Jess looked from the policemen to his fiancée. "I told Karen all about this before I called you. I didn't want her to be surprised."

"What happened then?" Mike asked.

"Well, I'd had enough. I told Rose that I felt sorry for her and didn't want to hear anymore. Before I closed the side door behind me, I turned to her and told her that if she changed her mind, just to give us a call. She picked something up and I barely got out the door before she threw it. Whatever it was, it made a loud crash. I could hear it outside."

"That must have been the figurine we found smashed on the floor," Mike said.

Sheski nodded his head in agreement. "What time was it when you left there?"

"About two-thirty. From there, I went back to my office and tried to work. However, as the afternoon went on, I started to feel ill. I was sweating and nauseated, so I stopped by Dr. Connors' office, got a prescription and went home and went to bed. That's why you couldn't get hold of me. After taking the medicine, I was knocked out for quite a while."

The lieutenants thanked Jess for his candor, informing the couple that they would probably have some further questions for them later.

Sheski and Mike got in their car and drove down the farm lane slowly. "I hope he's telling the whole story," Mike said to his partner. "It's obvious they love each other very much, and I don't think Karen could take the shock if Jess is our killer."

"I think you're right, but he does have a motive, and he can be placed at the scene of the crime." Sheski then added, "Call Sarah, Mike, and see if she can talk to us. It should be Dr. Stone's lunch hour about now. Maybe we can spend a little time with her. And call Debbie at the barracks and have her check out Jess's story about being ill and seeing Dr. Connors."

Mike made the calls from the car phone, which was now in working order. Sarah answered at Stone Haven on the third ring. "I was just saying good-bye to Dr. Stone. He has an appointment with Attorney Smithson about Rose's estate and will be gone most of the afternoon. Come on over. I have some time I can give you." She sounded pleased to be part of a clandestine investigation.

"We'll be right there," Mike told her.

Chapter Twenty-three

After parking in Stone Haven's front lot near a sign marked *Visitor,* Sheski remarked to his partner, "Ever notice that we don't see any clients milling around here? Lana told me that it's because the ones in residence have back doors they can use and there are private points of ingress for the day clients. The rear driveway can be accessed for their convenience, too."

"Nice and private," Mike replied

"That's what they pay for."

They entered the double doors and walked over to Sarah's desk, smiling. She was having a lively conversation with Shannon Albright, and the men were sure it wasn't about the four major food groups. Both women turned toward the men and grinned.

"Are you here to see me or Lana?" Sarah teased. "Lana's not back to work yet," she said, suddenly serious. "But you probably already know that. I hope she's all right. We're worried about her."

Sheski grinned in return and said, "She's doing fine. We're here to see you, for now. Can we go somewhere and talk?" He was hoping she would suggest Dr. Stone's office again. She did.

Once inside the office, they made small talk and then Mike got to the point.

"We need some more information, Sarah. You've been a big help so far. I don't know how we can repay you."

She raised her eyebrows and said, "I'm sure we can think of something." Both men looked at her quizzically and she laughed. "Oh, don't worry," she said. "I'm just teasing. Actually, I hope I can be of some real help to you in solving these horrible murders. I shouldn't be telling you this, but I knew Barry Brown. He was a client of ours. He always looked so sad, but he wasn't a bad person, you know, just a poor guy who was mentally ill. He didn't deserve to end up like that. I can't say the same about Rose, though. Now, what can I do for you today?"

"I'd like to take a look at Pratt's journal first," Sheski stated matter-of-factly.

"That's a big order," Sarah said cautiously. "I think I can fill it, though."

She went to the top right drawer of Dr. Stone's desk, took a key off her own key ring, and carefully unlocked it. She then reached her manicured hand inside and produced another key. Smiling, Sarah dangled the small, brass key in front of the two men. "This should do it," she said proudly.

"Where'd you get the key to his desk?" Mike asked.

"Don't ask," Sarah replied. She then went over to the glass display case, opened it, and carefully took out the Pratt diary. The large leather-bound book looked fragile. Loose pages were sticking out from the volume.

"I hope you know what you're looking for," Sarah said, placing the delicate journal on top of the table. "Because I wouldn't know how to begin finding anything in that old thing."

"I think I do," was Sheski's reply.

Mike watched as his partner gently opened the diary. Sheski lightly turned the pages, scanning them as he went, being careful not to cause any damage.

"It's incredible. I feel like I'm going back in time," he said.

Indeed, the notations were so vivid that the reader felt as if he were present during the recorded events. Pratt was a skilled writer, detailing each day's activities, the color of the sky, the weather, all as vibrant as one of his oil paintings.

Sheski was in a hurry to find specific information, so he couldn't be wasting time today reading just for the pleasure of it. If Dr. Stone came back, they would have a lot of explaining to do. He skipped ahead to right before the painter died. Sheski had learned that Dr. Burns's mother was a patient at the same time as Pratt. She was in the psychiatric unit of the Danville Medical Hospital from February, 1934 until June of 1938. That was where Sheski began reading. Skimming over the pages, he finally found what he was looking for. He soon became immersed in the skillfully-told tale woven by a twisted demented mind.

Not fully trusting Sarah to keep important information private, Sheski gestured for Mike to come read silently along with him. In flamboyant black script was an accounting of Pratt's joyous news of November 12,1937. It began.

Today is the happiest day of my life. My beloved Becky has given birth to our son. She came through the ordeal without any difficulty, despite being attended by just that midwife Anna. The old harpy wouldn't let me in the room with my love while she labored. Said it wasn't decent. She may end up having to pay for that. After Becky doesn't need her anymore. The little one is already sucking and looking around at the world. Maybe he will be a painter like his father. Oh, I hope he will be kind and sweet like my Becky. I was permitted to see our son when Anna went home for the evening. He has my love's beautiful violet eyes and the distinguishing Pratt mark. I only regret that I am no longer a young man. This child may have to grow up without knowing me. Today, I will finish the self-portrait that I have been working on so he will have something to look upon and know who his Papa was.

November 14, 1937. He is a beautiful baby boy. Somewhat small as I am but perfectly formed. I can't stop staring at him. My Becky is recovering well despite the neglectful care she receives at the hands of her attendants. If I live long enough, they will get their payback for that. We don't know what to do about raising this child. As I am writing this, the doctors are writing orders for his adoption. Shameful. I can teach him what he needs to know about getting along in this world. I am feeling weaker each day and fear what will happen to him and his mother once I am gone. My needs are unfulfilled these past weeks because of Becky's condition. Although I am feeling unwell, I still desire my favorite pastime. I am considering other ways of fulfilling my desires. Painting is all I have now.

The two lieutenants looked at each other, acknowledging that what they'd thought was true was fact. Sheski handed Sarah the journal and indicated he wanted her to put it back in its case. Sarah placed the journal in the same spot from which she had removed it, next to one of the monogrammed feeding cups. She cautiously replaced the brass key in the rosewood desk and locked the drawer.

"Did you find what you were looking for?" she asked expectantly.

Sheski assured her that he had. He added there was one final favor to ask of her.

"Sarah, we can't stay long, but we need to know where Dr. Stone was on the night Lana was attacked."

"You don't think he was part of that, do you?" she asked surprised.

"I don't know," Sheski answered, "but I have to check it out."

"Come on back to my desk, and I'll check his schedule."

Sheski and Mike were relieved to find themselves out of the psychiatrist's office. They felt vulnerable when they were there.

Sarah, puzzled expression on her face, replied, "Both Drs. Stone and Burns were here that night. I remember it now because it was the day of Rose's burial. I couldn't believe it when he called me in to do some work. He had a new computer program he wanted us to install. He made a big production out of it, but we finally got it accomplished. You wouldn't think that a newly-widowed husband would want to be working, but Dr. Stone insisted."

The two men thanked the receptionist, taking turns shaking her hand vigorously. "You've been a tremendous help to us, Sarah," Mike said. "We can't thank you enough."

Sarah, touched by their kind words, winked and said, "You know where I am, if you need anything else."

Back in their car, Sheski turned to Mike and grimly said, "So, John Deadly is Rebekah Burns's illegitimate son with Oliver Pratt. There was something about Deadly and Dr. Burns that was nagging at me. And something about the Pratt self-portrait that Deadly had hanging in his hallway. Both John Deadly and Dr. Richard Burns have their mother's violet eyes. Both

Oliver Pratt and John Deadly have a brown triangle-shaped birthmark above their right ear, the 'Pratt mark' that Oliver wrote about in his journal."

"No wonder Deadly could afford to have such a nice house and an original Pratt," Mike said. "He probably inherited all of Pratt's artwork."

"That also explains his obvious pride when I remarked on the Pratt paintings at Dr. Stone's house on Saturday," Sheski said. "I thought he was just boasting about his knowledge of art. In fact, he was proud of his father's talent. Wouldn't old Pratt be disappointed to find out that his son has neither his father's artistic abilities nor his mother's sweetness. He may have inherited some of his father's other personal traits, though."

"Did you put that call in to our contact in the Army?" Mike asked Sheski.

"Yes. He's supposed to call me back as soon as he finds something out," his friend answered. "Whatever he has for us could tie up some more loose ends."

Chapter Twenty-four

Over a late lunch at The Bridge Stop, the lieutenants began to unwind. Coffee and homemade soup and muffins were ordered. From their window table, they watched across the river as a swift-moving train gripped the tracks en route to an unknown destination. *New York?* Sheski wondered.

Conversation in the restaurant slowed as the train began to signal and could be seen from the windows. Boxcars swayed gently from side to side, noisily and swiftly chasing one another in a northeasterly direction. The pulsating sound carried well across the water.

The men were soon joined by Andy Wallace, who placed his lunch order. The three shared information on the murders. The local policeman made a lot of sense and collaborated with the investigators on their plans.

While drinking coffee, Andy placed a phone call to the District Attorney from his cell phone, obtaining more news. "There's an interesting twist to Deadly's association with the Burnses," he said to Sheski and Mike. "According to the D.A., Dr. Burns's father, attorney James Burns, handled Deadly's legal affairs from the time of his birth. The D.A. believes that the attorney, out of respect for his wife, saw to it that her son, Pratt's son, received the artist's paintings and meager possessions upon his death, including the self-portrait. He also arranged the legal adoption of her baby, days after his birth. The infant was placed with Joseph and Ruth Deadly, a local couple who had no children of their own. They named the baby John. His middle initial, P, was given to him by James Burns, at Rebekah's request. It stands for Pratt. It seems that the Burnses wanted the child in town, where they could monitor his welfare. Joseph worked at the iron mill and Ruth stayed home to raise their new son. The Deadlys made sure that their son knew at a young age that he was adopted, although they didn't know who his birth parents were."

"A psychologist would have a field day with the psychodynamics of the relationship between Pratt and Rebekah," Mike said thoughtfully. "A young woman suffering from postpartum depression and grief over a stillborn child develops a relationship with a much older patient, a child-killer, which results in the birth of another infant!"

"You're right," Sheski said. "But relationships between patients of all ages are not uncommon in psych wards. They reach out to each other for love and companionship. It happens all the time."

"Deadly must have done some checking around and

discovered the truth about his mother and father," Mike said.

"I guess so," Andy replied. "Anyway, the D.A. is researching files to see if Rebekah Burns made any settlement regarding her estate for Deadly. About your question to your Army contact about where Deadly was when Dr. Stone's mother had her accident. He called our office and left a message for you. He says you owe him big-time because some of this is top secret. At the time of Elizabeth Stone's auto accident, John Deadly was home on leave from the Army, right here in Danville. He also confirmed that Deadly's birthdate is November 12, 1937."

Sheski stared at Mike, his mind racing.

"And," Andy said looking grim, "It seems our boy Deadly was suspected of being involved in a case of some missing children in 'Nam. The Vietnamese police had an eye witness, one of the local men, who placed Deadly near the scene of the disappearance of one of the little girls, but they couldn't make anything stick." He paused a minute for effect, and then said solemnly, "Deadly's old friend, Lesley Stone, was his alibi."

For the first time in many years, Sheski was speechless.

The men talked a little more about the case and then Andy left, promising to continue investigating Deadly's legal issues. Sheski got up once in awhile during their meal to look out the window, across the river toward Lana's house. Her bodyguards kept him current on her whereabouts by cell phone so he knew she was still at home. After lunch, they paid the waitress and went out to their car.

"Do you think we could make a stop at Lana's?" he asked Mike while driving. "We're so close. I won't take too long." He needed to cleanse his mind of Deadly's repulsive activities with someone he cared for.

"Go ahead. I'll wait for you in the car," was his friend's reply.

"No, I want you to come in with me. It looks a lot better, what with neighbors and all."

Mike rolled his eyes at his friend's caution and nodded his head.

Sheski leaned against the car and called Lana. He didn't want to just pop in on her without advance notice.

"Hello," Lana said.

Sheski could hear Bunky in the background barking in response to the call.

"Hi there," Sheski returned. "Bunky sounds in good shape. I'm nearby and wondered if I could stop in for a minute. That is, if you're not too tired."

Lana brightened. "I'd like that. Ignore the way I look, though. I'm still pretty shaken up."

"You couldn't look bad if you tried," was the reply. "Do you want me to bring you anything?" he asked.

"I'd love to have some coffee, with cream."

"You got it. I'll be over in a few minutes." Sheski went back in, filled Lana's order, and with a lighter heart returned to the car. "Let's go," he said.

Mike watched Sheski brighten after his telephone conversation. He felt encouraged that maybe his friend was finally ready to start a new relationship. He drove the car across the bridge and parked in front of Lana's house.

Sheski rang the doorbell, and Lana opened the door dressed in blue scrubs. Her make-up looked freshly applied, but dark circles were still visible under her eyes.

"Hi, Tommy. Hi, Mike. Come on in," she said quietly.

From somewhere in the laundry room came shrill, welcoming yips.

The policemen said hello. Mike stayed leaning against the front door while Sheski took off his overcoat and followed Lana to the kitchen in the back of the house. The two looked at each other, smiling broadly.

Sheski handed Lana her coffee and they got comfortable on the kitchen chairs. He leaned toward Lana and asked attentively, "How have you been?"

"Okay. I'd be a lot better, though, if I knew who it was rummaging through my house and what they wanted from me," she said tightly. "I feel so violated, and I'm frightened to let Bunky out of my sight."

With that proclamation, Lana got up and released Bunky from his enclosure. He ran around the kitchen, under their chairs, and then, one by one, attempted to jump up on them. He finally managed to sit on Lana's lap while she drank her coffee.

"This is really good. My first cup today. I've been spending more time off the couch but still have a slight headache. I hope by tomorrow to get back to work. There's so much to do there. Dr. Stone has been working, business as usual, and I'm sure it's piling up on my desk. I guess it keeps his mind off of what happened."

Sheski nodded.

"Do you mind if we go into the television room while we talk? I feel like I have to lie down."

With that, Lana got up and led the way through the dining room and into the television room. Sheski watched her and thought, *My God, she even looks good in baggy scrubs.* She stretched out on the couch and motioned for Sheski to sit near her. Bunky followed his mistress closely, jumping up on the couch after she got situated. Mike remained quietly leaning on the door.

"Where're your bodyguards?" Sheski asked.

"One stays outside all the time, patrolling the grounds. The other one, Trooper Enterline, saw you coming and went outside for a few minutes. He said he'll come back in after you two leave."

Sheski was relieved to know the guards were being vigilant.

"Every now and then I still get a little lightheaded," Lana went on. "The doctor said that should start to subside in a few days, but for now, lying down sometimes feels much better."

"Can I get you anything else?" Sheski asked worriedly. Inside, he was fuming that someone could do this to her.

"No, thanks. I'll be all right. Bunky keeps me company and family and friends call and stop by to check up on me. They've brought enough food to feed an army."

With that, the little dog jumped down off the couch and started to pull at Sheski's right shoelace. Growling at an imaginary enemy, Bunky pulled at the black string and succeeded in untying it. Sheski playfully reached down to grab the dog but the Yorkie was too fast for him.

"Hey, stop that, young man," Lana yelled to her pet. Recognizing that he was being scolded, Bunky took one look at Lana and scrambled under the couch. They could hear him under there, struggling to get against the wall where he couldn't be reached.

"I'm sorry about his bad behavior, Tommy."

"He didn't hurt anything," Sheski replied, retying his shoe again. "I hope I didn't scare him, I was just trying to play along."

With that, they could hear the dog scrambling around under the couch again. There was a slight tinkling sound as if he was chasing after something, trying to get hold of it.

"I wonder what he has," Lana said quizzically. "Whatever it is, it isn't good. He's always making off with something. I have to watch him closely or he'll chew up whatever he gets his teeth into."

Bunky slowly slinked out from under the couch, furry little face first. Dust balls clung to his silky hair, and the Yorkie proudly pranced around the room with a metal object between his teeth. Knowing she wouldn't get it if she scolded him again, Lana said sweetly, "Come here, boy, come to Mommy. Let me see what you have." Bunky jumped up on the couch and, striking a self-satisfied pose, showed off his treasure.

Hanging from his tiny teeth was an 18-carat gold key chain with a single key and an attached gold disc. The letters *KB* gleamed brightly from the disc's center.

Lana managed to grab the prize from Bunky's mouth before he could get away. The dog tried to get it back, but Lana was holding tight.

"Who does this belong to?" she asked, furrowing her brow. "It looks really expensive. KB. . . . KB," she muttered. "Whom do we know with those initials?"

"May I see that?" Sheski asked, taking out a clean handkerchief to get it.

"Sure." Lana handed the article carefully to him. "Whoever lost that will be sorry. It's a very expensive piece."

Sheski looked it over. He frowned for a few minutes and then, suddenly, his jaw dropped, and his face reddened.

Seeing his surprised look, Lana asked, "What?"

"This must have been dropped by the intruder when your house was ransacked, Lana, and the police missed it when they were here. Bunky probably snatched it up and hid it under the couch before the owner knew it was gone. I bet I know what they were looking for, too."

"What?" Lana said, exasperated.

"The missing nine-carat diamond," he replied. "According to Karen, Rose Stone knew that her husband and Kylie Burns were having an affair. She even accused him of it during the big blowup on St. Valentine's Day. Karen told us all about it. So Kylie could easily be involved in this whole matter. Since the diamond wasn't with the other loot on Barry Brown's body, they must think that you have it, Lana. That you picked it up when you found the body. They couldn't bear the thought of losing such an expensive item. I remember what Bobby Snyder told us. He repeated over and over how much Lesley Stone loves money, never has enough. If that's true, the loss of that diamond must have really gotten to him."

Sheski looked down at the key ring in his hands, his mind reeling with this new evidence. "Kylie is the only one in this whole picture who isn't accounted for, at least not yet. We were with John Deadly when you were attacked, so we know it wasn't him. Drs. Stone and Burns were at Stone Haven with Sarah, providing Stone with an alibi, no doubt, so they couldn't have done it. But what about Kylie Burns . . . KB? Where was she?" he asked bitterly. "She could have surprised our officer who was guarding you, knocked him cold, and then lay in wait for you to come out of the house when Bunky barked. Maybe she even planned to break in and assault you. Whatever her plan, you did her a favor by stepping out onto the patio that night. She struck you, ransacked the house, and somewhere in her frenzy, dropped her key ring."

"I don't have the diamond," Lana said defensively.

"I never thought you did," Sheski said thoughtfully, touching her hand. His voice then hardened. "But Stone and Kylie suspected you. Stone probably promised to give it to Kylie sometime in the future. Barry Brown didn't have it on his body, so the murderer must have kept it. He planted the other jewelry on Barry's dead body and hoped everyone would believe that the ring washed down the creek. Evidently, Stone didn't want to believe it was lost. He also didn't want to believe that his partner in all this didn't have it either. He was hoping that you found it at the murder scene, Lana, and took it. So he sent Kylie to get it back. Since Kylie didn't find it at your house, Stone must be asking himself who has it."

"But how does Deadly figure into this?" Lana asked, looking puzzled. "Why would Dr. Stone align himself so closely to this man?"

"We have our ideas but will know a lot more after our meeting tonight."

"What are you going to do?" Lana asked excitedly.

"Mike and I will be meeting with Dr. Stone in a couple of hours. We asked John Deadly and Dr. and Mrs. Burns to be there, too. It should be very interesting. In the meantime, I want you to stay in the house, Lana. At least until we're sure you're out of danger. Our men will continue watching your place, so you can feel safe while you're here."

"Don't worry, I'm not going anywhere, the way I've been feeling."

The detective got up to leave and walked down the hallway to his partner, who was still waiting at the front door. Despite Sheski's protests, Lana accompanied him, opening the door for the men. Mike went out first and Sheski leaned against the inside of the door.

He inclined his big frame toward her and said gently, "I'd still like to cook that meal for you Saturday evening, if you're up to it and aren't busy."

"I'd like that," was Lana's reply.

"Great, I'll pick you up around six P.M. and we'll go to my place. You won't have to do a thing. I'll take care of it all."

He wrapped his big arms around her, pulled her close, her back to his chest, leaned down and gave her a soft kiss on the cheek. He nuzzled her neck and whispered into her ear that he'd see her soon. Then something clicked in his detective's brain. Not wanting to break the mood to reveal what he had just realized—that the killer had pulled his victims up close in a similar manner—Sheski held her quietly. Lana turned to face him, and rested in his arms for a minute before the detective said, "I have to get to work now. Keep your doors locked. I'll call you."

The first thing Sheski did upon getting into his car was to page the guard who was supposed to be inside the house with Lana. Upon the trooper's assurance that he had stepped back into the house, Sheski relaxed. The second thing he did was to place two more telephone calls. He spoke to the county judge to get the necessary legal paperwork and then asked Andy Wallace to do some searches.

He filled Mike in on their discovery, showing him the key ring. On their way, the two talked about how eager they were for the meeting tonight. It was a long shot that they were playing. Knowing who they were dealing with, they decided to chance it. Put it all out there so everyone could see what the others were up to, and watch it unfold. Their guests were all volatile, selfish people and anything or nothing could happen. Although they doubted the latter.

Getting everyone together was not an easy task. Each kept begging off with myriad excuses until the police made thinly-veiled threats about how they could be forced to attend. The lieutenants expected that attorney Smithson would make an appearance with the others, too, in the interest of his clients.

Sheski and Mike had agreed not to involve Karen or Jess in the meeting. Their presence would add another dimension of passion that was best left out. Depending on the outcome, those two could be advised or interrogated at a later date.

The lieutenants' calendars had to be cleared to provide enough time for the confrontation, in case there were any surprises. Sometimes these showdowns worked and sometimes they didn't. They weren't sure what would happen when their suspects were challenged and asked unwanted questions. The policemen knew that most of all, it depended on the character and personalities of the people attending. Self-assured suspects often bluffed it out until the end. But not always. Sometimes the more volatile ones broke down when faced with negative feedback from the others present in the room. The only thing they were sure of was their own strategy and that their quarries would each have plans of their own.

Chapter Twenty-five

Sheski and Mike drove into their office parking lot at 4:50 P.M. In forty minutes, the show would begin.

At 5:25, John Deadly arrived, followed by Lesley Stone, who was driving his Mercedes. A sober-looking Richard and Kylie Burns appeared a few minutes later. Stone and Deadly were greeted formally by Sheski and the two immediately seated themselves close to the door, next to each other. Both voiced a greeting to the Burnses when they entered the room, but did not extend hands for a handshake.

Deadly was wearing a blue uniform and his tam. As usual, he was also wearing his keys on a thick brass key ring dangling from his groin. He was, however, without a firearm. He didn't like the policy that all weapons carried by anyone other than state policemen must be surrendered to the trooper at the desk. He scowled when informed that his gun would be confiscated and returned upon his leaving. Deadly was accustomed to taking weapons from others, not yielding his own.

Dr. Stone arrived in a suit and tie, as did Dr. Burns. Both men wore white shirts. Lesley looked ten years younger than Burns, who appeared highly stressed. Violet eyes flashed behind Burns's round lenses. He kept brushing his long hair back from his face.

Kylie Burns was outfitted in her usual chic couture. This time it was khaki slacks, white blouse, and a black blazer with black leather flats. Her gold necklace, watch, and earrings were simple but expensive. A diamond pin was perched on her lapel and her medium-length red hair looked freshly done. She was anxious, which made her look much older than when the policemen had seen her playing happily with her dogs at her home. Today, she looked all of her fifty years and more.

Sheski was seated behind his desk, with Mike sitting on a chair to his right. Both men were wearing dark suits and ties and had Glocks in shoulder holsters. They appeared calm, but watchful.

"I hope we can get this over with soon. I have clients scheduled, starting with a six-thirty appointment tonight," grumbled Stone.

"I can't promise anything," Sheski replied evenly. "We'll have to see what happens here. Is attorney Smithson going to be joining us?" he asked of Dr. Stone.

"I haven't done anything wrong to warrant his presence," he answered firmly. The others nodded their heads in agreement as a testament of their own innocence.

At that point, Sheski's telephone rang three times.

He noticed the triple ring was an outside call and nodded to Mike to pick it up.

"Hello, Lieutenant Mike James speaking," he said professionally. When the person on the other end of the line identified himself, Mike looked over at Sheski and nodded his head in recognition of the anticipated call. After a few "okays," and "uh-huhs," Mike finally asked of the caller, "Is that all? Bring it on over." He hung up the phone and whispered something to his partner.

Sheski made eye contact with their four visitors, one at a time, and then began firmly, "I want to tell all of you that we brought you here to ask some questions, on the record, and to try to clear up some gray areas in our investigation of the murders of Dr. Stone's wife, Rose, and Barry Brown."

Mike proceeded to give the Miranda rights without a response from anyone. He made sure that they understood him and had no questions. Stone and Deadly betrayed no feelings that they may have been having, but Dr. Burns was fidgeting with his glasses. Mrs. Burns couldn't keep her hand off of her diamond watch, twisting it back and forth as if to assure its comfort on her slender wrist.

Sheski then took over. "We know that the two crimes are connected and were committed by the same killer. Frankly, we believe we can wrap up more than two murders today in this very room."

The four suspects looked at each other, unsure of what was to follow. "If you think I killed anyone," Kylie said curtly, "you're badly mistaken."

It was the opening Sheski was hoping for. "No," he

said, "You didn't kill anyone, but you very well could have." With a grim expression, he leaned forward in his chair and began.

"You know, Kylie, it has always bothered me that Lana's dog wasn't harmed when she was attacked and her house ransacked. Usually during break-ins where there's a family pet involved, it results in the animal's demise; even one as harmless as hers. So I asked myself, why did this trespasser tolerate Bunky, finally just locking him in an upstairs closet instead of bashing his little head in?"

Kylie's face drained of all color. Her expression turned grave and she grasped her black purse with white knuckles.

"I'll tell you why," Sheski said. "Because her attacker loves dogs, couldn't hurt one under any circumstances, and certainly not one as cute as Lana's. This intruder probably only locked the dog in a closet when he started to get too pesky. Someone with the initials *KB*."

He tossed the key ring down on the desk for all to see. "The same initials on this gold key ring the intruder lost in Lana's house. The same key ring Bunky found and hid under Lana's couch. *KB*. Kylie Burns!" Sheski's voice toughened and got louder. He was becoming angry over what Lana had gone through, so he paused a little so as not to lose his focus. "Someone who loves dogs, who spends enormous amounts of time rescuing and caring for unwanted dogs. Someone who owns a Yorkshire Terrier of her own. This is your key ring, isn't it! You were the one who struck the state policeman who was outside guarding Lana's house, and then Lana when she went out onto her patio."

Richard was looking at his wife in disbelief, waiting for her to deny it. Dr. Stone and John Deadly were giving her warning looks, willing her to keep her mouth shut.

"You can't prove it was me. That key ring could have been planted," she said angrily.

"We lifted a fingerprint of yours, Kylie, off the collar the dog was wearing the night you picked him up and placed him in the closet."

"He wasn't wearing a collar," she stood and shouted. And then, alarmed, Kylie realized that she had given herself away. "You tricked me," she said viciously.

"Don't say anymore, Kylie," Stone demanded.

Kylie sent a frightened glance to Stone and Deadly and sat back down in her chair. She was just beginning to realize how dangerous a predicament she was in.

"No, he doesn't wear a collar," Sheski agreed, his tone moderating, looking her full in the face. "Lana explained to me that Yorkies have a habit of getting themselves in all kinds of tight places, and she doesn't want to worry about her dog accidentally hanging himself. So, her dog doesn't wear a collar whenever he is indoors. So, you're right . . . he wasn't wearing a collar," Sheski said slowly. "And you knew that because you were there."

"What's going on here?" Burns demanded angrily of his wife, looking back and forth between her and Dr. Stone. "What is this about an assault, Kylie! Is it true?"

His wife didn't answer. Instead, she was looking pleadingly at Lesley, hoping that he would rescue her from the jam she was in. The rescue was not forthcoming.

"And Kylie," Sheski said, glaring at her, "you were the one following Lana on the bridge, too, weren't you? Wanting her to get jumpy and relinquish the Darling Diamond that you thought she had."

Seeing the guilty, scared look on his wife's face, Burns shouted at her, "How could you do such a thing?"

Kylie hung her head, covering her face, which was now streaked with tears.

Burns went on, "I knew you two were having an affair behind my back, right in our own place of business. But I thought you would come to your senses, Kylie. I thought you really loved me and this was just a passing fling, like all of Stone's other affairs."

He turned to Lesley and spat, "Can't you see what kind of a man he is, Kylie? He doesn't care about you. All he cares about is money. Ever since I've known him, he's always been about money."

"It's not like that," Kylie shouted back. "Lesley loves me. That's why I went looking for the diamond ring that night. Because he wanted me to. And we thought that maybe Lana had found it at the murder scene. She was the first one there. Maybe she picked it up. Anyone would have stolen that ring. It's beautiful and worth a fortune. He promised I could have the Darling Diamond when this whole thing about Rose blew over. He said it would be mine. That we would be married. Rose didn't deserve that ring. I did."

Richard stared at his wife in disbelief and scoffed, "Lesley wouldn't have given you anything unless he was getting something greater in return."

"What do you have to say to that, Dr. Stone? What could you possibly have gotten in return from Kylie?" Mike directed his remarks to Stone, who was shooting daggers at the Burnses.

"I'm not saying anything. She's lying. I had no part in what she did. I wasn't even there."

Kylie had heard enough. She lunged at Lesley, tearing at his face and clothes with her fingernails, screaming, "It was all your idea! You said we'd finally be together and have all the money we wanted. You promised that diamond to me!"

Lesley fought his lover off the best he could. She was hysterical, cursing and crying.

After a few seconds, Sheski and Mike stepped in to separate the two. Lesley's impeccable appearance was marred by scratches on his handsome face, his shirt ripped open, exposing his chest. He was breathing heavily and began dabbing at his facial wounds with a handkerchief. The doctor had gotten the worst of the row.

"The part about your not being there is true, Dr. Stone," Sheski said. "You made sure that you and Deadly had alibis that night, didn't you. Deadly was being interviewed by Mike and me. And you, Dr. Stone, made sure that Burns and Sarah were witnesses to your whereabouts."

"That's right," Dr. Burns exclaimed. "You made a big deal about the three of us installing that new computer program that night. Rose's body was barely cold.

Neither Sarah nor I wanted to do it then, but you insisted. We gave you your airtight alibi. You used me all the way around."

"I'm afraid he used more than just you and Kylie, Dr. Burns. He also used Deadly. Stone must have found out somehow that Deadly was Oliver Pratt's and Rebekah Burns's son. When in Vietnam, he also found out exactly how much Deadly had in common with his famous child-killer father."

"That makes you two half-brothers!" Kylie said incredulously, looking back and forth between Deadly and her husband.

With that revelation, Richard's face darkened. He covered his mouth with his hand and looked as if he was going to be sick. Deadly stared stonily at her, a sneer on his face.

Sheski went on. "Lesley may have read the Pratt journal prior to his Vietnam tour, did some checking, and discovered that Deadly's birthdate is November 12, 1937, the same date Pratt documented his son's birth. Stone was convinced of it, just like I was, after seeing Burns's and Deadly's violet eyes. Then there's the matter of the birthmark that Oliver Pratt had and said his infant son inherited. A brown triangle above the right ear. I saw it the night we were at your home, Deadly. On you and also on Oliver Pratt in his self-portrait."

The lieutenant had moved about the room while talking and was standing behind Deadly. He gave the tam a nudge, dislodging it from his head and onto the floor. Deadly cursed and lunged for the hat, but it was too late. The brown, triangle-shaped birthmark was revealed. Sheski eyed the blotch above the security man's right ear and went on.

"Stone then began to use his information to manipulate Deadly into doing some dirty work for him."

Despite the litany being recited, Lesley displayed no emotion. His keen eyes, however, bore into Sheski as he waited for the policeman to get to something he was interested in . . . something he needed to know.

Turning to Deadly once again, Sheski asked, "What could he have promised that would have convinced you to commit murder not once, not twice, not even three times but to be involved in four separate deaths?"

"Four, what four? There were only two murders," Burns rasped.

Sheski obliged. "Dr. Stone's mother, his wife, Barry Brown . . . and Samuel Stone."

Stone and Deadly sat still. Unnaturally still. As if the recitation not only did not matter to them, but as if it could not touch them.

Sheski began to unfold the murderous tale that their investigation had revealed. "The murder of Rose was planned the night she threatened to cut you out of her will, wasn't it, Lesley? And she was going to keep the Darling Diamond." He looked over at the psychiatrist, not expecting a reply.

"Rose was uneasy when Lana spoke with her on the afternoon she was murdered. Uneasy because she had a visitor she was frightened of. And with good reason!" He shifted his gaze to the security man.

"After Rose hung up the phone from talking to Lana, you were able to catch her off-guard and repeatedly strike her with the garden tool. Then she was in your grip, and you pulled her tightly to you as she died."

Kylie interrupted. "But what about Lesley's mother? She wasn't murdered. She died in an accident. Why would he want his own mother dead?"

"Tell them, Dr. Stone. Tell them how your mother planned on doing some good for her town. She was going to turn her entire fortune, including the sale of the Darling Diamond, into a charitable foundation. Lesley would have inherited only what funds were left from his father's estate. That wasn't enough for you, was it?" he judged, looking back over at the psychiatrist. "So, Lesley wanted his mother dead before she signed over all that money that he thought was rightfully his."

At this point, Sheski threw down on the desk a copy of the newspaper article recounting the death of Elizabeth Hastings Stone. Her beautiful, smiling face stared up at all of them.

"At first I couldn't figure out how you pulled this off, Deadly, since you were on active duty. So I did a little checking around. I asked my Army contact about where you were when Dr. Stone's mother had her accident back in July, 1968. He called back and we had a nice long chat. Besides giving us that info, he said he remembered you and some of your underhanded dealings in Vietnam. Said he knew that sooner or later you would be in serious trouble . . . again. He was actually pleased to know that a suspected child-killer may finally get his."

Deadly was starting to pay closer attention.

At the words "suspected child killer," the Burnses' mouths dropped open.

Sheski went on. "My Army friend tells me that you were on leave twice during your 'Nam tour. Once, at the time of Elizabeth Stone's auto accident, and the other when Sam Stone went into the river. Those are two big coincidences, Deadly. The way I see it, you intercepted Stone's mother, at Dr. Stone's direction, on her way to Catawissa. You put something in the road causing her to swerve, which resulted in her Rolls Royce crashing down onto the railroad tracks."

"You can't prove any of this," Deadly sneered.

"Oh, yes, I can. I can put you at the scene of each murder. There are some distinct similarities between the murders of all four victims, Deadly. Each of the four people you murdered had a similar bruise somewhere on their posterior. A large bruise on their back or shoulder blades, just about the size of a bunch of keys—like those you have on now, which you don't go anywhere without. Funny how you wear them, too. Most men wear them to the side or the back so that they don't interfere with whatever it is that they are doing. You wear yours on the front. Where they do get in the way."

Deadly looked self-consciously at the loaded key ring at the front of his belt, just inches from the buckle.

Sheski had gotten out of his chair and was leaning into Deadly's face. Eyes locked, he laid it on the line.

"Each victim had the same bruise. I know you're strong, black belt in karate, weight lifter. You're powerful enough to put your arms around each victim, pulling them close to you. There was a reason you pulled them tightly to you, wasn't there? What was it, Deadly?" He waited, but his prey said nothing.

"You see, it wasn't enough that you sent Stone's mother over the cliff. The police report noted that her body had been dragged out of the wreckage. They thought someone had witnessed the accident, tried to help her and then got spooked. But that's not true. You went down to the wreckage for another reason, didn't you? You got your arms around her from the back, pulled the dying woman close to you, and then what?"

Deadly began to sweat. Droplets rolled down his temples, over the birthmark and onto his collar. He wanted to tell them why he did that but knew he shouldn't. The others couldn't take their eyes off of him.

"What about Samuel? What part did he play in this?" Burns asked.

Sheski turned to Burns, then back to Deadly.

"I can piece most of that together from the police report and town gossip. Lesley probably tolerated Samuel's craziness right up until, in the manic phase of his bipolar disorder, his brother started squandering large sums of the family's money. Lesley had to find some way of stopping him. He didn't want to lose any of his precious wealth. Remember, Deadly is the only eyewitness to Samuel's death. And I don't think it happened the way he said it did. I believe that Samuel was lured to the river that evening and, mentally unbalanced, willingly went into the water. Samuel telephoned his brother that night and told him he was going to join his mother. Probably, Stone and Deadly had him believing he could reach her by plunging into the Susquehanna river."

Deadly and Stone looked at each other as if they were trapped. Stone was still preoccupied with something else.

He finally blurted out what was bothering him. "You think you're so smart, Sheski. If you're so almighty intelligent, where's my diamond? Who has the Darling Diamond?" he screamed, looking first at Sheski, then Deadly, then at Kylie. "It's mine, and I want it back." He then turned to Deadly and said viciously, "You have it, don't you. You're not only a killer, but worse—you're a thief. And I covered for you in 'Nam. All those missing children. Their families damn near beat the truth out of you. You're just like your father."

At this point, Stone got out of his chair and started toward the security man, who was ready to take him on.

Mike James, true to his reputation, was between the two before they knew what happened. He pulled Stone into a chair next to him, with the doctor trying to fight his way out of a wrestling hold. A split second behind him was Sheski, in turn restraining Deadly. The two men were placed in chairs at opposite ends of the desk and warned not to try it again.

"If you want to know where your precious diamond is, Dr. Stone, you will restrain yourself from now on, or I will do it for you."

Stone, breathing heavily from the altercation, nodded his head in agreement. "Where the hell is it?" he demanded again.

Sheski picked up the phone and rang an inside line.

"Is it here?" he asked. After getting an affirmative, he said, "Bring it in."

Andy Wallace came into Sheski's office, pulled a white handkerchief out of his pocket and handed it to Sheski.

Sheski delicately unwrapped the cloth, exposing the coveted piece of jewelry. All eyes were on the magnificent nine-carat diamond ring. The stone glimmered and shone, proudly displaying its priceless attributes.

The four suspects were poised to retrieve it, but, wisely, none made the move.

"You son of a bitch. How the hell did you get that?" Burns screamed at the officers.

Deadly turned to Burns and, seething, said, "So you're the one who stole it out of my locker."

"I deserve it, not any of you," Burns exploded. "For everything you put me through. I knew how badly all of you wanted that diamond. So, I figured I'd hit all of you right where it hurts . . . in your pocket. Make you pay for the pain you caused me. Having an affair with my wife right under my nose, Lesley. And you, Kylie. You make me sick."

He then triumphantly informed Deadly, "The ring wasn't really hidden well after all, was it, brother? I suspected you of murdering Rose all along. She was frightened of you, told me so herself, more than once. I thought she was just imagining things, but I guess she had good reason to be scared, didn't she? So, after her death, I decided to do a little searching of my own, looking for anything that would tie you to Rose's murder. All I had to do was get into your locker and look around. I waited until you were out on one of your little errands. Then I found it . . . in that old leather haversack under your security clothing. You took what I wanted, so I took something all of you wanted."

Stone looked at them and then at the ring. "I'm the only person with a claim to that diamond! It belongs to me. I didn't want to believe that you had double-crossed me, Deadly," he said, enraged. "I really thought maybe it had washed down the stream, or that Lana Stahl had it. Well, I want it back."

Stone lunged for the ring but, again, Mike was too quick for him. The officer made his move and got between Stone and Sheski, who was still holding the treasure. He then locked Stone's arms behind his back and pushed him down in his chair. Stone had been warned for the last time, and Mike quickly placed him in handcuffs, wrists behind him.

"We obtained search warrants this afternoon for all three of your properties, including Stone Haven, in an attempt to find the ring and any other evidence," Sheski said. "After talking with each of you and some others earlier, we had plenty of probable cause to present to the judge and he was happy to oblige. Andy Wallace dispatched men to search all those places after our informants assured us you were away from the areas. We made some interesting discoveries with those warrants," Sheski said, looking at the four suspects soberly. "The Darling Diamond was in your office, Dr. Stone, close enough that you could have gotten it whenever you wanted to."

Stone's face became crimson with rage.

"It was carefully tucked away inside an old hospital feeding cup in the glass display case, next to the Pratt journal. Very clever of you, Burns, to hide it in Stone's office. He would never have thought to look there. And if by chance it was discovered by the authorities, you figured that maybe we would believe that Stone had hidden it. But we knew better. Stone was still desperately trying to find the ring, so we knew he didn't have it. It had to be someone else."

Sheski carefully folded the ring back up in the handkerchief and stuffed it into his pocket.

"That's mine," exclaimed Kylie. "It was promised to me."

"Don't be stupid. That diamond is worth a fortune," Stone said roughly.

Kylie turned a venomous look on her lover.

"Richard is right, isn't he, Lesley? You had no intention of marrying me. You were using me just like you used everyone else." She looked over at her husband and then back at Stone. "I've been such a fool," Kylie said sadly. "I believed you. Everything you said. I even believed that once Richard was out of the way we would be together and share our fortunes."

"What do you mean, out of the way?" Richard asked, bristling. "What does *that* mean?" His voice rose and he sounded scared.

Sheski looked at them and said, "I'm not sure, so correct me if I'm wrong, you two. Deadly would soon have been been visiting Dr. Burns, and Kylie would have inherited everything. Then, by marrying her, Stone would increase his wealth even more. And

Deadly, who already had gotten a settlement from his claim to the Burns fortune, could have been rewarded with a percentage of that take. Money and a heritage he thought he deserved."

Sheski shook his head back and forth as if in disbelief. "And I'll just bet that's what they told you, Kylie, to get you to be part of the scheme. Stone probably convinced you that you would share in his wealth." He paused for a few seconds. "Anyone who really knows Stone says that he doesn't share anything."

"Share," Stone sneered, raising his voice. "Share! Share what? That was my money, mine. No one else deserved it. Not her." He nodded toward Kylie. "Not my mother and brother, either. Mother was going to waste it all. Give it away to charity. My own mother," he said incredulously. "She didn't even ask what I thought about that. Thought I'd be content with just Dad's money. What a fool."

Burns appeared overwhelmed by all that he was hearing. His face was outraged and, yet, puzzled. "But what about Samuel," he said uncertainly. "Your brother had his problems, but when he took his medicine, he was a decent guy. You could have kept him locked up and been guardian over his share. You didn't have to do away with him."

At this, Stone exploded again. "I couldn't count on it. My crazy brother was blowing tens of thousands of dollars on useless garbage. While I was away at college, he was home buying jewelry and stuff that he didn't need, and all kinds of gifts for the lowlife friends he met at the hospital. He was wasting our inheritance, my inheritance. I couldn't afford him," Lesley said coldly. "He had to go, too."

Kylie shuddered as she witnessed the depths of evil in the man she'd thought she loved.

Mike picked up on her anxiety and said slyly, "You know, if I were you Kylie, I'd have been watching *my* back, too. If both you and Richard were out of the way, there would have been no other heir to your estate. As a half-brother, Deadly could have contested his earlier settlement and walked away with everything. After all, he would be the only survivor to the Burns fortune."

Kylie slumped back in her chair, finally defeated. Tears were flowing and she was whimpering quietly to herself. Her husband stared at her with contempt on his face, realizing that he could have been Deadly's next victim, the next one to feel those keys dig into his back.

"Why did you pull Mrs. Stone out of the wreckage, Deadly?" Richard asked. "She was dying."

Deadly looked at his half-brother with disdain. Then he began, "Do you know what it was like living the way I did? I guess not. You with your Harvard degree, living in a fancy home off the family inheritance. While I had to live a life deprived of a legitimate background. My mother's family, prominent, wealthy, and thinking they're too good for me, embarrassed by me. My father a lunatic child-killer. I could feel your family's hatred for me, and so I nursed my own hatred right back at all of you. I vowed that someday they would pay for taking my mother away from me, for buying me off when I was just an infant, like a nobody, having to keep silent as a provision of the settlement," he said sullenly.

"And that bitch Rose. Yes, I went there that day to kill her. When Lesley asked me to do it, I was glad. I hated her. Always acting as if she was better than everyone else. She once called me trash, and I never forgot it. I enjoyed killing her, too. When I was done with her, she didn't look like much, did she?" He was enjoying the memory of their confrontation.

"Unfortunately for Barry, he was part of our plan, too. A pity. He was always nice to me. Barry was alive, you know, when Lana Stahl saw me in the garden," he said to Sheski. "That weakling was easy to overpower. I had him bound and hidden until she went in the house. Then I put him in his truck and took him back to his place. We walked together to the creek and I stuffed Rose's jewelry in his pockets before disposing of him. I kept the ring, though. I just couldn't bear to part with it."

"That wasn't the plan, was it?" Sheski asked. "You knew that was Barry's day to work at the Stones' property. Dr. Stone wanted you to put all of Rose's jewelry deep in Barry's pockets for the police to recover when his body was found. Then it would look like he had killed Rose and all of her diamonds could have been returned to him. But you got greedy, didn't you, Deadly?"

"I deserved that ring more than they did," Deadly said. "So I told Lesley that I must have dropped it at their home when I killed Rose, or maybe it fell out of Barry's pants at the creek. That I wasn't sure. That put him onto Lana Stahl and off my back. Someone had to pay for how I've been treated. Everyone trying to make out like I was nothing when I was just as good as they were. That's why I pulled them close to me before they died. I whispered into their ear and told each one of them whose son I was. That I was just as good as they were. Maybe better. Where they were going, they couldn't tell anyone, so I knew they would keep my secret."

Deadly's boastfulness then changed to a softer tone. "I couldn't help it, you know, killing those little girls in 'Nam. It's not my fault. That was part of my inheritance from my father. I shouldn't be held responsible for something I cannot control."

Sheski couldn't help himself. The murders of those children really bothered him. He just had to know the reason for it. His face looked pained as he asked the question to which they all wanted the answer.

"There was a war going on, Deadly. You could have had a belly full of killing. Legitimately. You could have killed off Viet Cong soldiers to your heart's content. Why murder little children?"

The room went silent. All eyes were on John Deadly. Eager for the answer, yet afraid of what the answer could be. They were not prepared for the shocking truth.

Deadly leaned his head to one side and looked disgusted at their stupidity. His softer tone gave way to a sinister reply. "Because I couldn't get my hands on their babies, that's why," he said matter-of-factly. "Parents are so careful with their infants. I couldn't get close to any of them. But their children have the run of the village. It was so easy, almost too easy to be interesting. Like my father, I was very good at getting them to want to be with me." He smirked and continued. "It was payback time for what had been done to me. I was just a baby myself when adults tore me from my parents. Took my heritage, my identity . . . everything was taken from me. Someone had to pay."

He could see that he had shocked them all. The expressions on their faces showed the depths of horror they were feeling. They didn't get it, the fools. He was justified in extracting his revenge. It wasn't his fault.

At this point, he started to laugh. "I enjoyed every moment of it, oh yes, I did. Daddy and I, we understand each other."

It was the first time that either lieutenant had heard him laugh. It was raw and biting. As if he alone was privy to some marvelous insight that others could never expect to understand.

Sheski looked at the four persons seated in front of him. "Each of you selfishly valued something that you wanted above all else. Even above human life. But there's one thing you forgot about the vermin like yourselves that you hooked up with. You forgot that your kind are not team players and will only ever really be looking out for yourselves. Every one of you thought you had manipulated the others and were going to get what you wanted."

Sheski tapped the interoffice button on his phone twice, and eight fully-armed state troopers entered the room. Two positioned themselves in front of each suspect and proceeded to place them under arrest. Surprisingly, there were no escape attempts. And there was no escape to be had. One by one, they were handcuffed and taken from the room.

As Deadly was being led away, Sheski leaned over and whispered in his ear. "That haversack we found ties you in to some monkey business you pulled on Bobby Snyder in Vietnam, too. When this is all over, he'll be glad to get it back."

Before Sheski could get out of the way, Deadly, grinning in defiance, spit full in his face. Fighting the impulse to slug the smaller man, Sheski wiped his face with a handkerchief and said to the staties, "Get him out of here."

Chapter Twenty-six

Lana was dressed in a casual black jumpsuit and black flats when Sheski came to pick her up for their date. Her dark hair was pulled back from her face, and around her neck she wore a simple gold cross. He kissed her lips gently as they sat in the front seat of his car. They then drove to his house in Lewisburg. After a quick tour, he escorted his date into the dining room and seated her on a cloth-covered chair. Yellow candles in silver candlesticks were lit, and he began serving the promised meal.

He placed chilled forks on the yellow and blue color-coordinated cloth napkins, and served each of them a crisp watercress salad with vinaigrette dressing.

"I'm impressed," Lana said, smiling up at him.

"Wait until you taste the bouillabaisse, standing rib roast of beef, and bourbon-soaked chocolate truffles," he said, grinning.

Lana looked at her handsome host in his dark slacks and white shirt, blue half-apron draped over his lap, and asked, surprised, "Where did you ever learn to cook like this? This is fabulous."

Sheski shared with her his depression after the death of his wife and his lack of desire to engage in social activities. He explained how Mike, out of desperation over his friend's grief, enrolled the two of them in cooking classes at a local college and browbeat him into going.

"Mike eventually got bored and dropped out," Sheski said, "but it was good therapy for me. I became hooked and stayed on. I still take classes sometimes."

Lana took a few bites of the fresh watercress and said impishly, "I could get used to this."

Sheski took her hand, and she rose up out of the chair. Pulling her close to him, he looked into her clear green eyes, kissed her full on the mouth, and said, "I hope so, darling. I hope so."

Epilogue

Due to plea-bargaining and testimonies of the defendants, neither a coroner's inquest nor exhumation of bodies long dead would be necessary.

Barry Brown's missing truck was eventually found in the river, where Deadly had disposed of it.

Dr. Richard Burns would not face charges for his possession of the Darling Diamond, and, clearly shocked by the full extent of his wife's involvement in the crimes, willingly provided evidence against all of the accused. Through his attorney, he swiftly served Kylie with divorce papers.

Kylie Burns, crushed by the knowledge of Dr. Stone's plans against her, also plea-bargained to avoid a long prison sentence. She was placed in a program for first offenders and given six years' probation. She eventually gained the state's approval to move to Philadelphia, where she now works at an animal shelter.

Dr. Lesley Stone, in an attempt to avoid the electric chair, pleaded guilty to his part in the deaths of his mother Elizabeth, brother Samuel, wife Rose, and Barry Brown. He also was cooperating with the United States Army, Vietnamese officials, and local police in their investigation of John Deadly. Stone was sentenced to life imprisonment without parole in the state penitentiary at Rockview. His precious money was turned over to his daughter, Mrs. Karen Walter.

In an attempt to capitalize on his famous Pratt heritage, John Deadly tried to plead innocent, due to insanity, of the murders of six Vietnamese little girls and four Montour County adults. The District Attorney, however, countered with a full examination by a state psychiatrist, who found him sane and capable of standing trial. While in jail awaiting trial, Deadly surprised everyone by hanging himself in a basement cell, using a prison bed sheet flung over a ceiling light.

The notorious Darling Diamond is scheduled to be sold, again, at a Christie's auction next month. Because of this latest grisly chapter in its history, the gem has generated interest from wealthy collectors all over the world. Proceeds from the sale will go to a charitable foundation in the names of Elizabeth and Samuel Stone.